He held out his hand for the tire iron

"You want me to give it a try?" JT asked.

"I can manage."

"Now you're being unfriendly," he said, smiling the sweet, slow, dimpled smile that, coupled with the laugh lines around his eyes, added up to the most disarming, charming, wiseass expression Hailey had ever seen. "What's the use of growing up in a garage if I can't change a tire for a beautiful woman every once in a while?"

When she still hesitated, he said, "Look, Hailey, that car is old and the nuts are probably rusted. It's a question of muscle, not know-how." He paused and then added, "You can pretend I'm not me, if that helps."

If only she could. But there was no way, because she was quickly realizing she hadn't forgotten one detail of his looks or his voice or his smile....

Dear Reader,

How much do we really know about the people we love? Hailey and JT, the main characters in *The Boyfriend's Back,* grew up together, dated each other, shared a secret and changed the course of each other's lives, but did they really know each other? Do they want to? When JT comes back to town after a fifteen-year absence, they're going to find out.

I was interested in writing a "coming home" story where the impressions and labels the characters have been carrying since childhood are becoming uncomfortable. What does it take to break free of the expectations of friends and family without breaking those lifelong bonds? What is important enough to hold on to no matter what?

I'm delighted to let you know that this book is the first of two about the McNulty family and their hometown. Take a good look at JT's little brother, Charlie. He'll be starring in his own book coming in December 2009.

I hope you'll enjoy *The Boyfriend's Back.* Extras about the book, including behind-the-scenes facts, are on my Web site: ellenhartman.com. I'd love to hear from you! Send e-mail to ellen@ellenhartman.com.

Ellen Hartman

THE BOYFRIEND'S BACK

Ellen Hartman

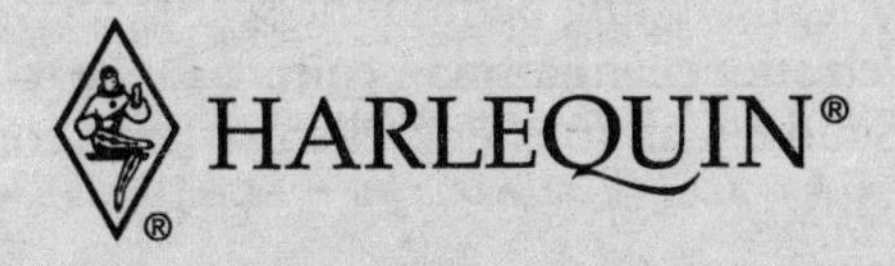

TORONTO • NEW YORK • LONDON
AMSTERDAM • PARIS • SYDNEY • HAMBURG
STOCKHOLM • ATHENS • TOKYO • MILAN • MADRID
PRAGUE • WARSAW • BUDAPEST • AUCKLAND

Recycling programs for this product may not exist in your area.

ISBN-13: 978-0-373-71563-3
ISBN-10: 0-373-71563-3

THE BOYFRIEND'S BACK

This edition published by arrangement with Harlequin Books S.A.

www.eHarlequin.com

Printed in U.S.A.

ABOUT THE AUTHOR

Ellen has been making a living as a writer since she graduated from college and went to work for Microsoft writing documentation for Word. She took a year off in the mid-1990s in order to write the Great American Novel, but instead she played a lot of Frisbee and planned her wedding. She currently lives in a college town in upstate New York with her husband and sons.

Books by Ellen Hartman

HARLEQUIN SUPERROMANCE

1427–WANTED MAN
1491–HIS SECRET PAST

This book is dedicated to my mom and dad.

At its heart, this is a story about family. My parents keep the traditions and connections of our family close. Loyal, supportive and always ready to babysit, they continue to find new ways to share their love with their family.

I would never have turned this manuscript in had it not been for my long-suffering writing friends Diana, Harriet, Leslie, Liz and Mary. They kept me going when I was sure it was past time to stop. Special thanks to Jeannie Watt, who allows me to send her panicked late-night e-mail and never fails to respond with wit and wisdom.

CHAPTER ONE

CHURCH, BAR, CHURCH, bar, Statlerville was exactly the same as the last time JT had been here. But he was lost. How did a person get lost in their own hometown?

Move away and stay away for fifteen years. That's how *he'd* done it, anyway.

Now he was late, which was just perfect. He was only coming because his brother, Charlie, said he couldn't do this without him, and now JT wasn't going to make it in time. He glared at the empty expanse of dashboard. Of course his rental didn't have a GPS—why use technology when you can keep right on making the same stupid mistakes forever?

He should never have agreed to this. But Charlie had asked him. JT rolled down his window and took a good look at the streets of Statlerville. Something would ring a bell—show him the way.

There. St. Pete's, his high school. His mom's funeral was being held at the Statlerville Volunteer Fire Department hall. Four minutes tops and he'd be there. Looked like he was going to be on time, after all.

HAILEY WAS IN THE MAIN treatment room at Viva, the rehabilitation and physical therapy center she ran, watching her first appointment of the day. Rita Temple, rehabbing after a hip replacement, finished her last set of lifts just as Hailey's cell phone vibrated in her pocket. She handed the checkout sheet to Rita as she opened the phone.

"Hailey?" It was Sarah Finley, her best friend, speaking in a barely audible whisper.

"Sarah, where are you? The opera?" She smiled.

"I'm at Melanie McNulty's funeral. Olivia's here." Sarah paused. "Hailey, she's sitting with the family."

Hailey stared blankly at the photo of Bing Crosby in *White Christmas* hanging in front of her on the wall of the treatment area. She couldn't make her brain process what Sarah had said.

Melanie McNulty had died three or four days ago; she'd missed a curve on Route 6 driving too fast in the dark. Hailey hadn't realized the funeral was today, but her daughter apparently not only knew about it, she'd decided to skip school to be there. With the family.

"I'm on my way," Hailey said before hanging up.

She asked the receptionist to reschedule her clients because of a family emergency—which was so ironic she almost laughed—and was putting the key in the ignition of her ancient Mustang convertible before she realized that she hadn't asked Sarah if JT was there.

But he wouldn't be, would he? He'd never come

back. She'd heard he never even spoke to his parents on the phone.

He *couldn't* be there, because Olivia *was,* and that was bad enough…but not unfixable. As long as JT wasn't there.

The funeral was already under way when she got to the hall. She had a clear view up the aisle at Olivia, who was wearing the navy sweater and kilt they'd bought for last Thanksgiving, the extra half inch of thigh between the hem and her knee a heart-breaking reminder of how fast her baby was growing up and out of childhood.

It was funny, Hailey thought a moment later, how she might not have recognized her daughter. Olivia's narrow back and tall-girl, teenage slouch looked unfamiliar only because she had one hand on the back of Jack McNulty's wheelchair.

Hailey's eyes moved next to the two tall, broad-shouldered men in dark suits standing next to Olivia. Charlie. And unmistakably JT.

JT McNulty was standing with Olivia. Olivia thought she was standing with her dad.

For one instant Hailey imagined hustling to the front and rushing her daughter out of there the same way she'd moved her away from the baboon cage during a kindergarten field trip to the Philadelphia zoo when the residents had begun a noisy round of monkey love. But she couldn't. Couldn't shelter her daughter from this now that Olivia was here. Couldn't pretend that her daughter hadn't lied and cut the last day of school to be here. Couldn't ignore the fact that Olivia was standing there with the McNultys just as if she belonged to them. As if they were part of her life even though, as far as Hailey knew, she'd never spoken to any of them.

JT MCNULTY HAD LIVED through a lot of jacked up drama in his thirty-two years. His parents had been reality TV—*The Biggest Spectacle* or maybe *How Screwed Up is Your Family?*—before the concept was even invented.

This funeral was vintage McNulty, he thought. The twenty-four-page glossy booklet he'd found on his seat was closer to a Playbill than a funeral program, and he was wishing like hell he'd stayed in Pittsburgh. He should have sent a really nice flower display and called it a day.

Last he knew his family was Catholic. But this didn't resemble any church service he'd ever been to, and Father Jordan's pissy attitude back at the funeral home finally made sense. Charlie had told him his mom had planned her funeral a few years ago after she'd been in the hospital overnight with chest pain. Calhoun's Funeral Home had pulled out those notes and this spectacle was the result. Of course this service wouldn't have been allowed at St. Pete's. The huge, black-bordered photos of Melanie hanging on the side walls, the program, the original poetry substituted for prayers—none of that would have flown in the church.

It was theater, not a funeral. Which he supposed he should have expected. His mom had never lived in the same world as other people. Hers had been full of chaos, the one constant had been Melanie's place in the center of the spotlight. And there she was again in the spotlight, on the video screen this time, which currently displayed one of the large nude self-portraits she'd done his senior year of high school.

JT couldn't watch. Instead he elbowed Charlie in the side. His brother half turned to him impatiently. "What?"

"Who's the kid?" he whispered. The dark-haired girl standing on the other side of Charlie had hugged Jack and then slipped into the chair next to him as soon as they got here. At first he'd thought she was a nurse, but when he took a better look he realized she probably wasn't old enough to drive.

Charlie shook his head. JT couldn't tell if that meant "later" or "I don't know, either" but he let it go.

"And finally, a few words from Melanie," the funeral director said as he hit a button on the sound system.

His mom's smooth, rich voice rolled out, accompanied by more video footage, and JT was startled by an unwelcome sting in his eyes and at the back of his throat.

He was here for Charlie. Not for her. But watching the old pictures and home videos scroll by as her voice filled the hall, he missed her. It was weird as hell that she was giving her own eulogy. She hadn't ever been much of a mom. At times she'd been out-

and-out awful. But she'd been his mom and she'd died and…

And he'd left things a mess with her. Never tried to repair what had been ripped apart when his parents kicked him out. The screwed up, not too happy times they'd had were all they were ever going to have.

God.

His dad made a sound deep in his throat and JT glanced over at him. Jack was a big man with a thick head of blond hair and he filled the wheelchair in a way that was awkward to see. JT had stumbled through greeting his dad that morning, unsure how to act around the man who'd dominated his childhood, but now seemed diminished.

Jack pursed his lips and JT had a moment of panic that he was going to see his old man cry. He swallowed and rolled the program tight in his fist. This was worse, way worse than anything he'd expected. He wasn't supposed to be getting upset about his mom or worried about his dad.

Then Jack cleared his throat and hocked a gob of spit a healthy distance out into the middle of the floor, close enough to the casket to make his intended target perfectly clear. The kid put her hand up to her mouth to cover her shocked gasp. Charlie was pretending so hard he hadn't noticed he was practically vibrating with the effort. JT clenched his jaw tight to keep from laughing. *Perfect.* His mom was driving his dad insane from the grave and the entire town of Statlerville was witness to the scene. Welcome home.

HAILEY'S STOMACH was queasy as she watched Olivia sneak peeks at JT. The expression on her daughter's face, hungry and excited and intense, was enough to tell Hailey exactly how much of a mistake she'd made. A good number of the other guests were watching JT and Olivia, too. Statlerville wasn't exactly a small town, but it was small enough, and insulated, as many of the suburbs of Philadelphia were. Hailey had grown up here, knew most of these people, and of course they were curious about JT and Olivia. They all thought they were witnessing the reunion of a long lost dad and his daughter.

While Hailey was practically a carbon copy of her mother, Olivia hadn't inherited either the famous Maddox beauty or her real father's distinctive green eyes. She had Hailey's dark hair and wide brown eyes, but the way her features came together was all her own. Based on appearances, she could be JT's daughter as easily as that of almost any man in the room.

When the service ended, the funeral director wheeled the coffin out of the hall, JT and Charlie walking behind it. Olivia was just behind them, still with one hand on Jack's wheelchair. JT glanced at his brother and back at his father, but then stared straight ahead, not meeting the curious looks from anyone on either side of the aisle.

Hailey moved back from the doorway, tucking herself close to the wall. JT didn't notice her as he went past, following Charlie out into the sunlight.

When Olivia came through the door, Hailey reached for her wrist and pulled her close. Jack stopped his chair and watched them.

"Mom, let go."

"Stop it, Olivia," Hailey said.

"No, you stop it. You have to let me go." Olivia pulled backward, her eyes on the doorway through which JT had disappeared.

Hailey tightened her grip, conscious that other people were starting to file out of the hall. She leaned closer and said in a low voice, "No."

Olivia threw a glance over her shoulder, but Jack was now surrounded by other people and his sons hadn't come back inside. "I just want to see him," she said. "We didn't get to talk. He didn't even say hello." Olivia's brown eyes were full of hurt as they locked on Hailey's, looking, perhaps, for answers.

As her skin flushed first hot and then cold, she realized how serious her mistake was. What had she done to her girl? She'd never meant to hurt Olivia; she'd lied to try to avoid the hurt. All she'd wanted was to give her daughter what every other well-loved child had. But she'd messed up.

Before she could respond, JT was back, moving through the crowded entry toward his father. Olivia pulled her wrist free. Hailey barely registered the greetings from people she knew as she witnessed this first encounter between her daughter and JT.

He'd grown into his height, was more solid but still handsome. His dirty-blond hair—chunky dark tones liberally streaked with lighter gold—was swept back off his forehead in a more contemporary version of the surfer-style mop she'd found so endearing when she used to watch him sleeping through English class. His lanky form had filled out, too. His suit jacket clung to his shoulders and stretched across his back, testament to lean muscle underneath.

Olivia stood frozen, her hands clamped on the sides of her skirt. Hailey reached the wheelchair at the same time as JT.

His eyes widened in surprise. "Hailey?" His voice was low and he hesitated over her name.

"I..." She stopped. "I'm sorry about your mother."

"Thanks," he said without emotion. He barely seemed to see Olivia before he glanced down at his dad. "The car is waiting to take us to the cemetery." Before Hailey could think of anything else to say, he'd grabbed the handles of the wheelchair and was pushing Jack toward the door.

Olivia was standing perfectly still, clearly shattered. Hailey met her daughter's eyes before Olivia fled out the side door.

Hailey started after her, trying not to shove people, but using a little muscle. When she made it through the side door and onto the sidewalk, she saw Olivia waiting next to the Mustang. Hailey slowed her steps, closed her eyes and said a quick prayer of thanks.

Olivia was quiet in the seat next to her as they pulled out of the parking space and started down the street. Her face was bent forward, hidden by the curtain of dark hair.

At the first stop sign, she lifted her head slightly. "I just wanted to see him." Her voice was so whisper soft Hailey almost missed it. Tears prickled in Hailey's eyes.

"I understand," she said as she made the turn onto Main.

Olivia's shoulders hitched as she tried to hold back a sob. Hailey could no more have kept her distance than she could have juggled chainsaws. She reached awkwardly over the console and put an arm across Olivia's shoulders. Rubbing gently, she murmured, "I'm sorry."

It's my fault.

Olivia put her head back down, hugging her abdomen as she cried. "I wanted to see him. Because you don't talk about him and I never saw him except in your yearbook and I didn't know if I'd ever have a chance again."

"I know, baby," Hailey soothed. "I know."

"But I..." Olivia stopped talking as another set of sobs shook her shoulders. "I couldn't say anything...and why didn't...why didn't he even *say hello* to me? I was right there and I couldn't say anything and he didn't even say hello."

Hailey closed her eyes. This was exactly what she'd wanted to avoid. This exact scene with her daughter reaching out to someone who didn't want her. Hailey couldn't believe the lie she'd told to avoid this was now the catalyst for it.

"Shush, Olivia, honey."

Just ahead she spotted an open parking space on the shady side of the street, and she pulled in. Olivia was still hunched over next to her and Hailey squeezed her shoulder.

"I have to tell you something."

Olivia stilled, her shoulders tense as she waited.

Hailey took a deep breath and then blew it out. She was having trouble getting enough air. She took another calming breath and then, for the first time in her life, admitted out loud, "JT isn't your father."

"What?" Olivia sat up, flipping her hair back to reveal her blotchy, tearstained face.

"He didn't speak to you because…because he's not your father." That sentence screamed for another half but Hailey wouldn't, couldn't finish it. Not now. Not ever.

"He is so my father. Everyone knows that."

"I let people think that. But it's not true."

"He sends me birthday cards."

"I send those."

"You…" Olivia paused. "Why would you do that?"

Because Olivia's real father had sworn he'd never have anything to do with her. Because it seemed safe. Because more than anything Hailey had wanted Olivia to grow up happy.

"I thought it was better. For you to have JT. Even though it wasn't true." When she'd sent the first card, she'd been angry. Some child in preschool had made Olivia cry because her dad wasn't coming to help pass out the cupcakes for her birthday. Hailey'd reacted in anger and didn't think it through.

The next year was harder because she did question what she was doing, but she sent the card anyway because it didn't seem that dangerous. JT hadn't been home in more than five years by then. His return seemed a remote possibility, separate from her and Olivia. And it was nice to think maybe JT was out there, still not taking his responsibilities seriously, but thinking about Olivia and sending her cards. She hadn't been in love with him when they were dating, but as time passed, he'd solidified in her imagination as a distant, slightly aimless dad for Olivia—infinitely preferable to the real thing.

After that, every year JT stayed away made it easier. Soon enough the card had become just one more little ritual, like using the clown-shaped candle holders on Olivia's birthday cake every year. Hailey bought a card, signed it from JT and slipped it in with the other gifts and envelopes.

Her daughter's dark eyes searched her face and Hailey held still.

Please don't ask it, please don't ask it. She worked to keep her expression calm. But of course Olivia asked. Anyone would have.

"Who is my dad?"

Hailey crossed her hands in her lap. "I…not JT."

"Mom!" Olivia's voice was an outraged whine. The childish tone gave Hailey the strength she needed to do what she had to do for her daughter.

Lying had been wrong, but she wasn't going to make the additional mistake of telling the truth.

"I can't tell you that."

"What do you mean, you can't tell me? It's my father," Olivia said. Then her mouth twisted. "I can't believe you lied to me about this. My whole life is a lie."

"I should have told you about JT sooner. I'm sorry." She paused and then continued. "If you want to talk, I…" But she couldn't finish. The one thing Olivia would want to talk about was the one thing Hailey wasn't going to discuss.

Olivia's hands were clenched in her lap. "You ruin everything." She pushed the door open and stepped out of the car. "You know, Mom, you're the one who makes such a big deal about trust." Olivia's voice rose into the mocking pitch teenagers knew instinctively how to use to such painful effect. "'It's just the two of us, we have to trust each other.'" She continued in her normal voice, "And you haven't been honest with me about *this?* About my dad?"

"Olivia, there were reasons."

"Sure there were." She glared at Hailey. "There are always reasons why you twist stuff. You can't let anything just be. You always have to change it, to make it better, perfect. But this isn't perfect and I'm never going to forgive you."

Olivia slammed the door and Hailey sat in the sudden silence alone in the car.

CHAPTER TWO

JT WAS RUNNING ON RESERVE battery power now that the post-funeral brunch at Reardon's Restaurant was winding down. He'd flown in from Pittsburgh early that morning, preferring to travel at dawn rather than spend an extra night in town. Lack of sleep was catching up to him.

He wasn't surprised how many people had turned out for the service and the brunch. Statlerville was like that. Everybody who wasn't a neighbor of your parents had babysat you or knew your dad from Rotary. He was more surprised about a few people who hadn't come. Most of the guys who'd worked at his dad's garage his whole life had been missing. He wanted to ask Charlie about that if he had time.

Hailey had been there for the service, but hadn't turned up at the restaurant. He'd have liked to see her, but he guessed she didn't feel the same. He'd wondered about her all these years, how she was, what she was doing. But she must have moved on long ago. Good for her, he supposed. Still. He'd have liked to see her.

In the past four hours he'd developed a new appreciation for his little brother. From his gray silk pocket square to the soles of his Alden shoes, Charlie looked every inch the businessman he was, every inch the anal control freak he'd been since the days when he'd kept their Legos sorted by color and size. More than just being physically polished, though, Charlie was poised. The man was a master of funeral small talk and, in a reversal of their childhood roles, JT had stuck to him like a semicoherent, sleep-deprived shadow.

Hoping to avoid getting entangled in any more conversations, he ducked out the front door to stand on the sidewalk. A few lingering guests were talking to one another in the parking lot, their voices loud and cheerful. Normal. The real world didn't give you much time to recover from a funeral.

JT turned his back. He hadn't expected there'd be anything for him to recover from. He was still shaken by how much his mom's voice had affected him.

He wasn't stupid. So why had he gone along assuming there'd be some warning before she died? Instead when the call from Charlie came, Melanie had already been dead and anything JT might have wanted to do or wanted to decide not to do was pointless. Typical of his relationship with his difficult, dramatic, demanding mom. Except that wasn't true. For once Melanie had not planned the drama. She hadn't meant to miss that curve and skid off Route 6 into a tree.

Charlie pushed the door open behind him and waited while their dad wheeled his chair out. His brother's face was tired now, too, the dark blue of his eyes almost black with weariness. He'd shouldered all of the work of dealing with the funeral home and making the arrangements this week, and it seemed to be catching up to him.

Charlie put his hands in his pockets as he walked over. That was a danger sign JT recognized. His little brother only ever pretended to relax during his most uptight moments.

"Dad, we have to talk," Charlie said.

Jack stopped his chair near JT but didn't make eye contact with either of his sons. Charlie spoke quickly, his voice nervous. "You need someone to stay at the house with you."

"Out of the question," Jack snapped.

"There is no question—it's a fact. The house isn't set up for a wheelchair. You had enough trouble when Mom was there to help."

"I can take care of myself. That's why I told that woman you sent yesterday not to come back."

"I'll come again tonight, but after that you have to have someone with you. You can't keep firing them."

Jack pointed a blunt-tipped finger at Charlie. "You hire another nurse and I'll make sure she quits before your check clears the bank."

"Dad, please."

Charlie sounded so tired that JT wanted to back him up, but he didn't know what to say. Jack would have no problem making life a living hell for a nurse. If his dad dug his heels in there was no way they could overrule him. Still, JT couldn't ignore the old impulse to watch his brother's back.

"Dad, Charlie's trying to help."

Jack looked straight at him. They'd barely exchanged six words since they'd met up in the funeral home that morning. JT had been half holding his breath, wondering if Jack was going to disown him or punch him or say something to indicate that the last time he'd seen him had been the night he kicked him out of the house for good.

This quiet, assessing stare his dad gave him now was unsettling. JT knew what his dad saw in him, the same thing he'd always seen. His disappointing older son. The kid who'd worn the mascot costume at the high-school football games instead of the quarterback's jersey. The kid who wouldn't try harder, wouldn't compete, wouldn't accept his authority and who'd picked his pregnant girlfriend over the future his parents had mapped out for him. JT hated that it was so hard to resist studying his feet when his dad turned that stare on him.

"Been a long time, JT."

"Yes, sir."

"You planning to stick around?"

"No, sir."

Jack held his gaze. Then, his mouth firm as he nodded a dismissal, backed his chair up and wheeled it around, only to stop briefly at the top of the ramp leading to the parking lot.

Without turning his head, he said, "Charlie, you want someone to stay with me, you get your brother to do it."

With one firm shove, Jack got the chair moving again and was quickly down the ramp and on his way to the car.

"Please tell me we have another brother I don't know about," JT said.

The corner of Charlie's mouth lifted in a weary half smile. "Jack McNulty, King of Contrary."

"*He* kicked *me* out. Am I the only one who remembers the whole 'if you're going to be a pig-headed fool you can do it someplace else besides under my roof' speech?"

"JT, come on."

"What?" The word exploded out of him with a force that surprised him. How had he let his dad rattle him this badly in such a short conversation? Not even a conversation, rather, two questions, a loaded look and an ultimatum. God, this day sucked.

"Ignore him. He's screwing with you. I'll stay with him tonight and then I'll get something sorted out."

"But why would he even say that?" JT asked. He wasn't sure if he wanted an answer, so when Charlie shrugged, he was half-relieved. He was acting like an imbecile. Like he was still the stunned seventeen-year-old kid he'd been that night when his parents had closed the door on him. It didn't matter what Jack's reasoning was. JT had a life. He couldn't stay here just because his dad asked him, no, ordered him to.

Charlie put one hand on his shoulder, squeezing and then letting go. "I appreciate you being here, JT. I'm glad you made it."

That simple touch from his brother slid a door open in his defenses and the whole day slammed home. His mom's voice, his regret over lost chances. His brother standing with him on their home ground. His dad as complicated as ever, messed up physically, mentally—who knew what was going on with him? But he'd said he wanted JT home. If JT walked out now, when would he come back again? Jack's funeral?

Was that what he wanted? The person he wanted to be?

"I missed you, too," JT said and then he stepped in and hugged Charlie—a full hug, not the manly chest bump Charlie was more comfortable with. He really had missed his brother. They'd made an effort not to lose touch despite his nonexistent relationship with their parents. Met up a couple times a year, went to Vegas for Charlie's birthday every June. But this felt different. He was in Statlerville. Home. He thumped Charlie between the shoulder blades and felt an answering pressure.

JT stepped back, but realized if he tried to speak, Charlie would hear the emotion that had tightened his throat. He took off his jacket and rolled up the sleeves of his shirt, using those seconds to get under control.

He needed that control when he made what was no doubt the biggest mistake he'd made since he'd sold his Apple stock right before they brought out the iPod.

Although he found it useful at times to deliberately cultivate appearances to the contrary, JT wasn't, and never had been, an idiot. He knew this was absolutely the wrong thing to do.

It couldn't have been worse timing, with the uncertainties looming at RoboGen, the robotics company he owned. He and his partner had been locked in debate since January. Terrance had plans for expansion and was lobbying for the resources to pursue bigger projects, starting with a bid for work on a NASA project. JT was pushing back hard. He liked RoboGen just the way it was, and was hoping Terrance would come around to his point of view. They needed to make a final decision in the next few weeks before the window to apply for the NASA bid closed.

But this was JT's dad, his family, and that had always meant more to him than he was willing to admit. The last time he'd spoken to him, the man had told him to get out and stay out. Now he'd invited him back. JT couldn't walk away from that. Not yet anyway.

It wasn't as if he thought he and his dad were going to fix everything. But possibly just being together again would help salvage something.

He slung his jacket over his shoulder and said, "I'm here now. Might as well stay a couple days until we can get him squared away." He made it sound perfectly casual and normal. Just a guy hanging around to keep his dad company. Maybe they'd have a few beers and watch the game. Shoot the breeze.

"JT, man, your heart's in the right place, but this is Dad. You can't take care of him."

"Can't, Charlie?" JT shifted his weight, moved into Charlie's space just a bit. Enough to remind him that being the older brother meant he got to do what he wanted, when he wanted.

Charlie elbowed him back a step. "Give me a break with that big brother crap. What about Robo-Gen?"

"Terrance can deal for a while." If JT was secretly psyched to be out of the arguments for a short time, who was going to know? Staying a few days after the funeral would be expected, right?

"So you're going to babysit Dad and work on robotics design at the kitchen table?"

"It'll be just like I'm back at St. Pete's doing my homework. Except I'll actually do it this time." He slapped his pockets and found the keys for his rented Taurus. "I'm going to walk back to the funeral parlor and pick up the car. You take Dad home and I'll meet you guys there."

Charlie tried to object again, but JT was already moving, halfway down the steps headed toward Cedar Street. Calhoun's wasn't far—ten blocks or so.

"This is stupid, JT!" Charlie yelled.

"See you at home!" he called back.

HAILEY HAD GIVEN Olivia two hours, knowing if she started after her right away, her daughter wouldn't want to hear anything she had to say. She called Viva and had Debby, the receptionist, start rescheduling her clients. Then she called her partner, Cynthia, to let her know she wouldn't be in for the rest of the day. She stopped by the house, hoping to find Olivia but when she didn't, telling herself she really had just wanted to change. She took off the gray pants and chalk-blue-and-white striped blouse she'd worn to work, and put on the silky, brown, Empire-waist sundress with sky-blue ribbon trim and her new sandals.

Then she drove around, scanning the spots she knew Olivia liked to go. No luck. As she turned the corner near the high school, she heard a loud bang and then a flap, flap, flap from the back of the car, and the steering wheel jerked to the left. She eased over to the side of the street and got out, certain she knew what she would find. She must have angered someone somewhere, because she absolutely couldn't catch a break today.

HER FIRST INSTINCT WAS to walk away. Maybe the tire would miraculously heal while she was gone. Maybe the flat was a hallucination brought on by stress. Or maybe a troop of Boy Scouts would come by and it would coincidentally be National Auto Shop badge week and they'd change the tire and fix whatever it was that caused that irritating squeal in the left windshield wiper while they were at it. And before they left they'd thank her for the opportunity to Do Good.

Or maybe it was time for her to grow up and face facts. Wasn't that part of what she'd done wrong with Olivia—hidden from the facts? Wasn't that part of her behavior she needed to change if she was going to earn back her daughter's trust? The tire wasn't a problem. It was a gift. A cosmic sign. Once she'd faced this reality head-on and handled it successfully she would know she was okay.

Right.

Fix the tire.

Easy. Except it was turning out she wasn't as in tune with the cosmos as she'd hoped. Starting with the fact that her sundress and sandals were not exactly "working on the car" clothes.

So what? She needed some practice in dealing with facts, not trying to change the situation to suit her. This was a good thing. A Life Lesson. No big deal.

Hailey took off her lightweight cardigan, folding it on the front seat of the car. In the trunk she found the fleece blanket Olivia used on cold mornings in the winter, and wrapped it around herself, tying it sarong style at the side. That would keep her clothes clean.

Even with the awkwardness and uncomfortable warmth of the blanket, it didn't take her long to get the spare out or to unfold the jack, which upped her confidence. She was reasonably sure she knew what she was doing. Take the flat tire off, put the unflat tire on. The cosmos wouldn't send her a sign she couldn't handle, would it?

Setting the tire iron on the first lug nut, she was surprised when she couldn't budge it. Leaning on the tool, she put some muscle into it. Nothing.

Settling more firmly on her heels, Hailey leaned on the tire iron with everything she had. Not even an encouraging squeak.

Did everything have to be impossible?

She reached back and slid her right sandal off. Gripping it tightly, she took careful aim and then smashed it repeatedly on the tire iron. As she smacked the shoe down, she whispered in a fierce cadence, "I. Lift. Weights." She shifted her grip and banged again, more desperately now as she realized the lug nuts weren't intimidated by her or her shoe. "Come off, you stupid car part."

"WD-40, look out. There's a car whisperer in Statlerville."

The man's voice startled her and she dropped her sandal, because of course it was him. No one, not even Owen Wilson, drawled in that pseudo-surfer, half-ironic tone like JT McNulty. Of all the people in the universe, he was the one who strolled by? He didn't even live in Statlerville. Hailey closed her eyes. She was all for cosmic signs, but this was out of control.

"You want a hand?" he asked from somewhere fairly close behind her.

"No, thank you."

She turned slowly and stood in one motion, not

wanting him to tower over her—no use being five-foot-seven if you couldn't equalize the power dynamic with a man every once in a while. "Hello again, JT," she said, wobbling on her one sandal.

He hadn't known it was her. That was clear from his step back and nervous swallow. Seeing her unsettled him, which was saying something because JT prided himself on his ability to take life as it came. Or at least he used to. She really knew nothing about the man standing in front of her. Except that the way he wore a suit made her pulse hammer as fast as it ever had over his Levi's back in high school.

"Hailey," he said, recovering his poise. "Didn't know that was you. Your, um, skirt thing threw me off." He gestured at the blanket, which she quickly untied as she groped with her bare foot until she found her shoe. If it had been someone else she might have made a joke, but it was *him* and she didn't know what to say.

She couldn't tell if he'd heard anything about Olivia. Did he know people thought he was her dad? Would he care?

The best thing would be if he could just go back to wherever he lived while she figured out how to handle her daughter. Then he'd never have to find out the mess she'd made. "No need to stay now that you know it's me."

"What does that mean?"

"Just that, if you had known, I imagine you would have walked on by."

"Huh," he said.

And wasn't that remark about as inscrutable as the cosmos.

He held his hand out for the tire iron. "You want me to give it a try?"

"I can manage."

"Now you're being unfriendly," he said, wrinkling his nose and smiling the sweet, slow, dimpled smile that, coupled with the laugh lines around his eyes, created the disarming, charming, wiseass expression she'd watched him wield with great success on everyone from teachers threatening detention to waitresses in the Statlerville diner. "What's the use of growing up in a garage if I can't change a tire for a beautiful woman every once in a while?"

When she still hesitated, he said, "Come on, Hailey, that car is old and the nuts are probably rusted. It's a question of muscle, not know-how." He paused and then added, "You can pretend I'm not me if that helps."

If only she could. But there was no way, because she was quickly realizing she hadn't forgotten one detail of his looks or his voice or his smile. The chances of him walking away while someone was having trouble were next to nothing, and she couldn't face struggling with the tire with him watching. Besides, she had the feeling he was right. She could hammer with her shoe or her fists and it wouldn't make an impression on her stupid car. So she wasn't giving up. She was making a mature decision and using the resources available. She handed him the tool, carefully keeping her fingers from touching his.

"Thank you," she said.

"Anytime," he answered as he looked for a place to put his suit jacket. She held out her hand and he gave it to her, then crouched by the flat. "Can't believe you're still driving this piece of junk," he said, half to himself. "In fact, I can't believe this piece of junk is still running, period."

He used to call the Mustang a chick mobile, telling her she should have asked her dad for a real car, not this pansy piece of junk. But he'd also adjusted the brakes for her when she'd complained about them, and taught her how to check the oil. He'd never seemed to take himself any more seriously than he took anything else.

He wasn't exactly dressed for the job, either, she thought as he set to work. His white dress shirt was untucked and the sleeves were rolled up past his elbows. She smoothed the back of her hand across his charcoal jacket where it lay across her arm. It was still warm from his body and she forced herself to stop stroking it. On the inside breast pocket she glimpsed a tailor's label with his name embroidered in red thread. Who'd have guessed JT would grow up to be a guy who had his suits handmade?

She was idly wondering what he'd been doing to be able to afford that kind of suit when he pressed forward to apply pressure to the tire iron, and the muscles in his back and arms flexed under the shirt. She tried to look away, but couldn't quite. Who could blame her? As a physical therapist, she worked with bodies and knew when one was put together right. In her professional opinion, JT was in…excellent…shape. If this was another test—a temptation this time—she wasn't anywhere close to passing.

JT's looks hadn't ever been model perfect, but his long nose and generous mouth were more appealing than they would have been on someone with less character. He'd always been more Abercrombie than Calvin Klein. His graceful, big cat physicality was mesmerizing. She hated that she noticed the slightly paler, vulnerable strip of skin at the base of his hairline above his collar. Hated that she noticed the way the light dusting of blond hair on his forearms caught the sun reflected off his platinum watch. Hated that she was jealous of that watch as the links slid across the tan skin of his slender, supple wrist.

Shivering, she felt a ball of heat in the pit of her stomach, even as she was irritated with herself. Just because she'd been basically celibate since her last unsatisfactory date with the son of one of her patients two years ago was no reason to start salivating over a man's strong, competent hands. Even if she knew exactly what JT could do with those hands. Even if she could still remember how good they'd felt on her a million years ago when she'd stopped him short every time because she'd been young and stupid and totally wrong about what she needed.

Hailey closed her eyes and thought *Uncle*. No

sense pretending she wasn't beat, when she so clearly, thoroughly was.

"Well, what do you know," he said as he turned the tire iron. His forearms rippled deliciously with the movement. "Your whispering loosened these bad boys right up."

He whirled the iron as she stayed silent behind him. She couldn't believe they were doing this. Standing on the street talking about lug nuts when there was so much between them that they'd never talked about. So much he didn't even know.

"Are we pretending I'm not me?" he asked with his familiar self-mocking humor.

"No." She smiled despite herself.

"'Cause if we were I could talk about the weather. But if we're not… How come you didn't come to the brunch?"

"I'm sorry about your mother," she said, before she realized she'd already told him that. He dipped his head but didn't say anything. That strip of skin at the back of his neck captivated her, reminding her of how much she had loved tangling her fingers in his thick hair when they were pressed together in one of those desperate high-school necking sessions. Did grown-ups ever make out like that?

She'd always stopped JT before they went further. She'd been so invested in appearing to be "Hailey the good girl," and JT was her public boyfriend—the one she shared with her friends and her real life. The things she did with Trevor Meyers,

Olivia's dad, were separate, secret, not part of her when she was with JT.

She looked away from his hair to the dusty roof of the Mustang. "It would have been awkward if I'd gone, JT."

AWKWARD DIDN'T EVEN BEGIN to cover it, he thought. This right here was a freaking fiasco, thank you very much. He flipped the iron to the next nut, glad he didn't have to concentrate on what he was doing, since being this close to Hailey and talking to her again had him all kinds of twisted up.

When would he learn that he didn't have to help every person in the world? So he'd seen a woman struggling with a flat. So she hadn't been dressed right for the dirty job. So he'd been rotating tires in his dad's garage before he started shaving. So what? He should have walked right on past—could have called McNulty's Garage from a safe distance and had them send a truck over.

He needed to be at his house, talking to Charlie and figuring out what was up with his dad, not on his knees next to Hailey's seventeen-year-old Mustang, having a stupid conversation with the only woman he'd ever proposed to. Who'd turned him down then the same way she'd tried to turn him down just now.

One of these days he was going to wise right the hell up.

"Awkward because we haven't seen each other

in fifteen years?" he asked. "Or awkward because the last time we were together I proposed and you said no for reasons you never actually made clear?"

Okay. So he was apparently not getting smart *today*. God. Seemed like this was the day he was going to pick at every single hurt hanging around from his freaking *childhood*. He gave a harder, angry twist to the tire iron.

At least Hailey had the grace to ignore him. In his peripheral vision, he could see her long, tan feet, red nails gleaming in black sandals with the kind of skinny sexy straps that would give even the most white-bread guy a foot fetish. She'd always had impeccable taste and a perfect understanding of what suited her tall, toned body. If he turned his head, he'd be able to see her incredible legs below the hem of that silky, impractical sundress. He didn't turn his head, though. He might be stupid, but he wasn't a masochist.

He hadn't realized she'd never left town. Figured, though. When they were kids he'd been drawn to her partly because Hailey and her perfect life had seemed the polar opposite of the craziness that swirled around his own family. It stood to reason she'd found some picture-perfect guy to marry, and was living the same kind of life here in Statlerville that he'd always imagined for himself.

He got the second nut off and moved on to the third. Right when he thought maybe he was going to finish the job without any more awkward conversation, she answered his question.

"You were seventeen," she said. "That wasn't enough of a reason?"

What the hell being seventeen had to do with anything he didn't know. She'd been eighteen, but just a few months older than him, and she'd been the one having a baby. He'd only wanted to take care of her and the kid.

"So, if I'd been nineteen, you'd have said yes?"

She didn't answer that, but then, she didn't have to. He'd stopped thinking she loved him a long time ago.

"Besides," she surprised him by saying, "we barely knew each other."

"We went out for most of a year."

"You didn't know me," she said softly.

That was an understatement. He grunted as he threw his shoulder into the stubborn third nut. When the tension gave suddenly, he slipped forward and caught himself with his right hand on the curb. The sting in his palm combined with the sting to his ego. He slapped the ground as he looked over his shoulder at her.

"You know what? Forget I said anything. I'm officially pretending I'm not me. You can do the same until I'm finished. Being here is going to be hard enough without digging through our stupid history."

He saw her brown eyes widen. "What do you mean, 'being here'?"

"I'm moving home for a while. Taking care of my dad."

He hadn't expected her to throw a welcome reception, but the way the color drained out of her face wasn't only insulting, it was alarming. He let the tire iron drop, and stood, grasping her elbows to steady her. Except the feel of her, her skin under his hands again after so long, was anything but steadying. He felt as if his palms were on fire, pin-pricks of heat jumping from her arms to him. She turned paler still and he knew she felt it, too.

He forced his hands into his pockets. "What's wrong?" he said.

"Nothing. Nothing. It's just bad timing."

How did his coming home for a few days have anything to do with her? They hadn't seen or spoken to each other since the night she'd turned his proposal down and he'd left town. There was nothing between them. Except…

"Is this about your kid? That's it, right? People still think it's mine?"

"She," Hailey corrected. She seemed as if she'd been about to say something else.

"She." JT tilted his head, trying but failing to get a read on her. "That was her this morning, wasn't it?"

"Yes." Hailey shrank in on herself, her arms crossed in front of her chest as if she was trying to protect herself.

Holy hell. The kid had hugged JT's dad. She'd stared at JT through most of the service.

"Does she think I'm her dad?" he asked, his words coming hard in his suddenly tight, dry throat.

"Not anymore."

"Not anymore since when?"

"Since a few hours ago."

He turned back to the car, dropping to one knee heedless of his suit and dealing with the fourth nut with ruthless efficiency. He couldn't look at her. Couldn't stand to know this about her. How many lies had she told to keep that story alive all these years? How could she?

"JT..." she began, but then stopped. The silence was heavy and uncomfortable.

"You needed a cover story for your *parents.* That's what you said. You asked me to say it was my kid until you figured things out." He lifted the tire off and propped it against the back door. "But after you turned me down, I never thought..." He stood up. "God, Hailey. I never thought you'd keep lying. She's not my kid, and you of all people know that."

Bending down, he grabbed the spare and lifted it into place, keeping his eyes on the car.

"I—I know..." she said, before stumbling to an awkward silence.

"Why would you even want to say it, anyway?" JT asked. His chest was tight with anger and old hurt. She'd cheated on him, lied to him for months and then asked him for help covering up what she'd done.

He'd been so stupid in love with her he hadn't even thought twice. He'd given up his college fund for her. Given up his family for her. He'd begged her to marry him, to come with him and let him take care of her and the baby. But she'd refused. He was good enough as a cover story, but not good enough to actually want to be with. Good enough to be her lie but not good enough to be her truth.

He stretched back his hand, reaching for the tire iron, but she grabbed it.

"I can finish," she said.

"Hailey, it's two more minutes' work."

"I would like—" Her voice shook and she put a hand up to her throat as if that would steady it. He focused on the curb next to his feet. If she was going to cry, he wasn't going to watch. She pulled herself together, though, and said, "I would like to finish it myself."

He pushed himself to his feet and took his jacket back from her. Fine. She'd made it more than clear she didn't want him around fifteen years ago. No reason she should want anything different now. "It's all yours."

She didn't answer, but crouched, tucking the skirt of her sundress between her thighs, and got to work.

He leaned on the hood and watched a collie-looking mutt scratching itself on the front porch of the house in front of him. He kept his mind blank, his hands in his pockets and his legs crossed, even though it took everything he had to keep from jumping forward when she struggled with the jack.

They didn't speak until she'd finished stowing the tools in the wheel well, and shut the trunk with a slam. The collie lifted its head at the noise and then put it down.

She opened the front door and pulled a plastic

container of wet wipes out of the glove compartment. She took one and then offered the box to him. He pulled a wipe out, more to have something to do than because he particularly cared about having grease on his hands.

"Listen, Hailey, I don't know what the hell you've been up to, but I'm going to be here taking care of my dad. I can't let him think…what he thinks. I'm going to tell him. And Charlie." He wanted to add, "And everybody else in this town who thinks I had a kid and never sent a birthday present or showed up for a Tee Ball game." But he didn't. Because as mad as he was, he'd never been able to hate her, never been able to forget her. Stood to reason he wasn't going to be able to do those things now, either, so there wasn't much point in trying.

She met his gaze then and he felt as if he was right back in high school, sharing a stolen moment in the cafeteria or behind the gym with her. That same feeling that he could get lost in her eyes if she'd just let him in.

"I'm really sorry," she said.

He nodded, because he didn't trust himself to speak and there wasn't anything to say anyway. Or there was too much to say, but he didn't know how to say it and wasn't sure she'd want to hear it even if he could figure out a way to spit it out.

He watched her pull away. He didn't have to, he knew. It wasn't as if the tire was going to fly off or anything. She'd done a good job. She'd be fine. But he watched all the same.

CHAPTER THREE

SHE'D ONLY GOTTEN one block before she saw Olivia walking ahead of her. Her daughter was striding along with her arms swinging, still wearing the skirt and sweater she'd had on that morning, and it was clear from her posture she was still angry. Hailey drove past her and parked, then stood on the sidewalk waiting.

"Get out of my way," Olivia said.

"I'd like to talk to you."

"Well, I don't have time to talk right now."

"Olivia, please."

"No, you please, Mom." Her voice was rough with anger. "You've humiliated me. And if you don't get out of my way it's just going to get worse."

"Worse?" Hailey asked, even as her daughter detoured around her.

"Yes. Worse." A tear ran down next to Olivia's nose and she wiped it away angrily. "Because I made him a scrapbook. Like an idiot. Because I believed you. And I put it in his car and any minute now he's going to find it and then he and everyone else will know about this stupid fake life I thought I had with a dad who never existed."

Hailey could barely think straight. JT was on his way to his car. "How did you know where his car was?"

"I watched him at the funeral home before the service started."

"Okay. I'll get it. You go home and I'll get it." As much as she'd rather not see JT again, she really didn't want her daughter running into him. She was not going to think about Olivia skulking around the funeral home that morning—the number of things she didn't know about her daughter was multiplying at an alarming rate.

Olivia stopped walking. "Fine," she said. "You do it. But this doesn't mean I forgive you. It just means I'd rather you be humiliated than me."

As she watched her daughter walk away, Hailey thought she'd deserved that. But at least she could do this one thing to help. Take a step toward healing or at least toward preventing further hurt.

She turned the car and went back, passing JT when he was still two blocks away from the funeral home. She didn't look at him, hoping he wouldn't notice her car as she passed.

In the parking lot behind Calhoun's she pulled into the spot on the right of a dark green Ford Taurus with an Avis rental sticker on the license plate. It had to be JT's.

She peeked in the passenger side window of the rental. There on the backseat was the scrapbook, a navy-blue cloth-covered book with a brown polka-dot grosgrain ribbon tying the pages shut. It couldn't have appeared more innocent, lying there like a snake in the grass.

She opened the door and grabbed the book. As she straightened, she saw JT walking down the driveway from the front of the building.

Instinctively, she ducked into the car. But as soon as she'd pulled the door shut, she let out a frustrated groan. Her instincts had led her to the exact opposite of the right decision. She was trapped inside his car with him heading right for her.

She ducked down, hoping he'd left something inside the building and would need to go in to get it. One of the Calhouns might call him in for a conference. Or he could get heatstroke and pass out. She'd call 9-1-1 from the street, she swore, if only he could lose consciousness long enough for her to escape.

She jumped when JT opened the front door.

His eyes widened as her saw her over the seat back. For a horrible, awkward moment, he stared. Then he ducked out of the car, to look right to her Mustang and left to the empty parking spaces before leaning in again. "Is this my car?"

Hailey shrugged. "How would I know?"

JT stepped back again, pointing first to her Mustang then to his rental, the only two cars in the lot. "See, that's your car. I recognize it because I just now changed the tire on it. I still can't believe it stayed on the road all these years. But whatever."

Could she bolt? She was wearing heels, which weren't really a good choice for a getaway, but if she ran he wouldn't chase her, would he?

"So that's your car, which means this must be my car." He sounded as if he was talking to himself, puzzling through a word jumble in the Sunday paper. "Granted, it's also a piece of crap, but renters can't be choosers, especially not at the crack of dawn o'clock in the morning."

There'd be no reason for him to chase her if she ran. In fact, he sounded so confused he might think she'd been a figment of his imagination.

"But here you are. In what I'm sure must be my car." He focused on her again.

She should have run. But she had missed the window. Instead, she opened the back door and got out, now on the other side of the car from him, holding the scrapbook next to and slightly behind her hip as she said over the roof, "I have a patient. Who has a wheelchair. And she wanted to know if a…" She leaned back to read the name on the trunk of his car. "If a Ford Taurus had enough room in the backseat for a wheelchair. So I was passing by and saw it parked there and thought I'd check it out."

His mouth wasn't exactly hanging open, but the expression on his face was as close to "you're insane" as she'd ever seen.

"Are you stalking me? I mean, I'm pretty sure we had a conversation about the fact that you just recently corrected your daughter's assumption that I'm her dad, and now you're sitting in my car…" When he closed his mouth a muscle in his jaw twitched.

She was tired and worried, and Olivia had really hurt her, and Hailey hated that JT was making it sound as if she'd lied about him all on her own. As if he hadn't agreed to it before she ever told anyone that Olivia was his.

"You said it was okay," she said. "I asked if you'd say you were the father and you said *okay.* You were there when we told my parents. Your parents were there. We did it together." She knew even as she said it that it wasn't fair. Technically true, but not fair. He *had* agreed, though, and she needed to hold on to that.

"No." JT squared his shoulders and pointed a finger at her. His eyes flashed. "You asked for my help until you were ready to tell your parents who the dad really was. *That* was what we agreed to. I never said anything about forever. I never agreed to lie to your *kid.*"

"Well, I never got ready to tell them."

"You better get ready, because as soon as I tell my dad, the story's going to get around."

"My folks are dead," Hailey said.

She saw hurt wash over his face, shadowing his eyes, and he suddenly appeared exhausted. She remembered then where they were and why he'd come home, and she was ashamed all over again.

She turned to her own car and got in, slamming the door shut behind her. She didn't look at him as she pulled out and headed down the street toward her house.

HE DROVE SLOWLY through Statlerville to his father's house, where he parked behind Charlie's black Mercedes and dragged his duffel out of the trunk. The lights were on in the kitchen of the rambling Victorian he'd grown up in.

Statlerville was an old town and his neighborhood had wide streets with big houses set on lots covered with huge trees. He lived in a very similar neighborhood in Pittsburgh and realized now for the first time that he may have chosen it precisely because it reminded him of here. Of home.

Most of the houses on his dad's street were well kept and he supposed Chez McNulty was, as well. Except, like all things McNulty, there was more than a hint of crazy. No one could deny that Melanie had an excellent, if dramatic, sense of color, so the eleven different shades of purple she'd used on the house worked. It was just that eleven was approximately eight more colors of house paint than anyone else on their block had used.

He took a deep breath and a quick check around the yard—not that he really expected to see Hailey lurking anywhere, but he'd had just about as many reunions with her as he could handle for one day. Then he went around the house and up the back steps to the porch.

Three cases of beer were stacked near the screen door beside a cooler. His neighbors knew how to take care of the grieving family, that was for sure. He opened the ice-packed cooler, grabbed a Yeungling, twisted off the cap and took a deep swallow. The coldness of the beer made him shudder. At least he pretended it was the beer that ran icy fingers down his spine, and not that he was on his own back porch and the second half of his round trip ticket to Pittsburgh was currently expiring in the bottom of his bag.

He glanced in the window. His dad and Charlie were there, at the kitchen table. Looked like they were settled in for a while. Looked like he was really doing this. Going home. He lifted the bottle and took another long pull, then tugged open the lilac-painted back door.

CHARLIE STOOD when JT came in, shoving his chair across the slate-gray tile floor. "We just sat down," he said. "There's stuff if you want something. People brought…" He gestured vaguely at the pans, bags and trays lining the black granite countertops. "I don't know what half of it is, but there's got to be something you like."

JT nodded, staring blindly at the food as he gave himself a second to adjust to being here, inside this house again. He'd never meant to turn his absence into a vendetta. Hell, right after he left there'd been more than a few times when he thought about crawling home. But he hadn't and gradually he forgot about it. Well, forgot how.

The kitchen was a dark, moody spruce now, not the eggplant it had been when he lived here, but otherwise not much had changed. They'd never been a dinner-at-six kind of family—the kitchen had seen way more use as a staging area for his mom and dad's parties than as a gathering place for their family of four—but it still smelled like home.

He dropped his bag by the door and reached for a plate. He really was hungry. A pan of lasagna was open so he took a slice of that, grabbed some bread and dumped salad and a spoonful of green beans beside it. Compared to the cooking he did for himself—more often than not takeout he microwaved in the staff room at RoboGen—this was a feast.

He sat across from Charlie, with his dad on his left at the head of the table. It all felt so familiar and so strange at the same time. It was like the day after he pulled an all-nighter at work, he knew how to do everything but felt as if he was living in a haze.

Nobody said anything for a few minutes. JT ate quickly and nervously swallowed the rest of his beer. The empty chair at the other end of the table was an oppressive reminder that his mom had died. He couldn't blame his dad for being on edge. His folks had been married for thirty-four years and they'd dated during college before that. Their relationship had been tempestuous, dramatic at its best and fiercely hurtful in the bad times. JT knew about one affair—his mom and Trevor Meyers. He'd have bet decent money there'd been others.

But for as long as he could remember it had been Melanie and Jack at the center of each other's lives. He knew how hard it was to adjust to life on your own. Still, understanding some of what his dad was going through didn't make him feel less uncomfortable. And it sure didn't stop him wishing he'd never agreed to come home. Especially now that he knew his dad and Charlie and everyone who shook his hand today thought he'd completely ignored his own child for a decade and a half. They must think he was a total dirtball.

Charlie grabbed a bakery box filled with cookies and brought it and a cake to the table, putting them down within their dad's reach. "People went overboard with this stuff," he said. "I don't know what we're going to do with all of it."

"I'll take care of it tomorrow," JT offered. He'd freeze some for his dad. Find someplace that took donations for the rest.

"I have to go in at least for the morning—work piled up," his brother said. "But I can probably get away early. I'll stop by and we can talk."

"All right," JT replied. "I'll hang out here and then we can get things straight."

Charlie nodded. "It'll be complicated, but I guess we can figure something out."

JT started to answer when Jack broke in. "I'm sitting right here. You have anything to talk about, spit it out."

Charlie's color rose. "I don't think you should be reminding people of spitting, Dad."

Ignoring that remark, Jack said, "Nice of you to come, JT."

JT couldn't tell if it was an accusation or an honest thank-you, and he didn't know what to say anyway. He shoveled a big forkful of cake into his mouth.

"I saw you talking to Hailey," Jack continued.

Charlie looked sharply at their dad but JT

couldn't read anything on the older man's face. God, this well and truly sucked. Whatever the hell had possessed him that morning, thinking he might come home and find some way to breach the years he and his dad had missed?

He hadn't even been here for an entire meal and Hailey was between them, right where she'd been during that last fight when his mom had said, "Choose" and he'd said, "Hailey," and that was the end of that. All those years his parents never got in touch, was it because they thought he had this kid and he'd never done anything for her? But that couldn't be it, because they were the ones who said he shouldn't throw his life away on Hailey and a baby they weren't convinced was his.

"There were a lot of people there."

His dad pressed his lips tightly together in an expression of impatience JT recognized from his childhood, and pushed his chair back from the table. "Don't know why you came home now. Too little, too late if you ask me."

"You're the one who said you wanted me here." He could have kicked himself for letting his dad get to him. Jack was one of the few people who could make him lose his temper.

The silence that followed was so full of tension JT was surprised it didn't set the neighborhood dogs barking.

"Just because I prefer you over some stranger your brother hired from God knows where doesn't mean I actually want you here."

Jack wheeled himself out of the kitchen and down the hall toward his office off the living room, leaving his sons in an embarrassed silence. Charlie lifted his beer bottle in a toast. "Just like old times, huh, big brother?" Then he started clearing up the remnants of their meal. JT grabbed his plate and his dad's. He crossed the room to Charlie, who turned to lean on the sink.

"I'm going to tell you one more time," Charlie said. "You don't have to do this."

JT shook his head. "I checked out of the hotel."

"They'd let you check back in."

"I've thought about this, Charlie, different times. What it would be like, you know? Coming home." He opened the dishwasher and stuck his plate in, and then started grabbing silverware and glasses from behind Charlie, out of the sink. It seemed as if it had been a few days since anyone had done any cleaning. "When I thought about it, she was here. So I have to try this. While *he's* still here. I need to find out."

"Find out what?" Charlie asked.

"Hell if I know," JT said. "Something."

Charlie tipped his head back and laughed. "You're still as screwy as you were when you were a kid. God, JT. How can you possibly run a company?"

JT opened the back door. He didn't want to talk about RoboGen. Wouldn't mind taking a vacation from thinking about RoboGen, in fact.

"You want another beer?"

Charlie nodded and JT grabbed two bottles from the cooler. He held the door open as he twisted the caps off and handed one to his brother. The evening air was cool but not uncomfortable. "Feel like tossing the Frisbee?"

Charlie glanced up at the sky. "Tell me you didn't pack a Frisbee."

"Come on, Charlie. I always pack a Frisbee." He leaned down and picked up the battered white disc he'd left on the porch earlier. "Go deep."

Charlie shook his head, but loped off down the yard and then turned to grab the catch one-handed. He tossed it back and JT jumped off the back porch to snag it.

They passed the Frisbee back and forth a few times, falling into a rhythm. Then Charlie started edging back after each catch, stretching the distance and making the throws harder. JT let it go a few turns and then yelled, "You move any farther away and you're going to strain something trying to heave it back up here!"

"Can't make the distance, huh, JT?"

Which was exactly why he and his brother should never play sports together. Charlie couldn't enjoy anything unless he figured out a way to keep score. All JT wanted to do was mess around in the yard with his brother and a Frisbee. Still, he hadn't been playing Ultimate half his life for nothing. He whipped the Frisbee down the yard and heard Charlie suck his breath in when it stung his fingers. Charlie's return was a little to the left but JT jumped, spun and caught it between his legs. His return throw was high, but Charlie caught it left-handed behind his back.

"We done with that?" JT yelled.

"Wimp!" Charlie called back. But his next toss was steady and right at JT's chest. After Charlie settled down, they lofted the disc back and forth, letting it float up and down the yard as they enjoyed their beer and the company. The beer, the growing dark, being with his brother… It all got to him and JT knew he had to tell Charlie the truth about Hailey's kid.

"I saw Hailey after the brunch," he said. "Helped her change her tire."

Charlie didn't respond, which pissed him off. It had been hard enough to work up to putting that first sentence out there, and his brother couldn't throw him a bone?

JT put some extra zip in his next throw as he tried again. "Were you planning to mention that my kid was at the funeral?"

Charlie had to jump to make the catch. "Hailey's kid." He cocked his wrist, said, "If that girl is yours, I'll eat this damn disc," then whipped the Frisbee back.

JT was surprised that the heat in Charlie's throw was matched by the heat in his voice. His little brother valued his ability to keep his emotions in check. He didn't sound so very in check right now.

Reflected porch light bounced off the silver on the label as he turned his beer bottle in his hands.

"I admitted I was the dad back when it all happened."

"And if you want me to keep pretending I believe that, I will. But I don't believe it and haven't for a long time."

"You don't think she's mine?" That was a relief. At least one person in Statlerville wouldn't have him down for Deadbeat Dad of the Year.

Charlie came toward him laughing. "Get real. I know you. If you had a kid, even one whose mom didn't want anything to do with you, you'd have been here. All the stuff you did for me when we were kids, and I'm supposed to believe you'd run out on your own baby?" He smacked JT's shoulder. "You remember Mom went on that granola-and-homemade-yogurt kick when I was in second grade? You stole money from the garage every day for a month so I could buy a school lunch."

JT dropped the Frisbee and they settled down on the porch steps.

Charlie swigged from his bottle. JT studied his brother's profile. Charlie's belief in him meant a lot.

"I didn't care if you got teased," he said. "I was worried you'd starve. Worried we both would. That granola freaking sucked."

"Dad was so pissed when he figured out you were the reason the register kept coming up short. I thought he was going to kill you. Thank God Mom went back to ignoring our lunches."

Charlie smiled. JT ducked his head. "I didn't know Hailey was still telling people that I'm the dad."

"What?"

"I mean, I lied about it. We both did. But she said she needed some time, that she'd tell her folks the truth as soon as she figured out how. I thought she would have straightened it all out a long time ago."

"She really screwed you, didn't she?"

That was the trouble, though, JT thought. She never did screw him. She'd had sex with someone, sure enough; the kid was living proof. But that someone hadn't been him. They'd come close, but he'd backed off because...well...mainly because she said no. He'd never gotten his fun from talking girls into stuff they didn't want to do. But in his mind, too, Hailey was better than that. He'd thought she deserved something special.

There was a part of him that had been scared of her, of how perfect she'd seemed. His parents had been in a really rough patch his senior year and he had taken advantage of the lack of parental oversight to go more than a little wild. Maybe his messed-up high-school self thought he deserved Hailey's rejection.

Judging by how she looked today, she was still perfect. Even when he'd caught her hiding in his car, she still seemed polished and put-together. Intimidating. Except now he knew she'd been a liar all along.

"How come you never said anything about it? Her. The kid," JT asked his brother. "You knew everyone thought she was mine. Didn't you think I'd want to know?"

"I thought you *did* know. I was there when you and Mom and Dad had that last fight, and I heard them telling you to admit that Hailey might have slept with someone else. But you wouldn't. For a while I thought the kid was yours. But then when you never asked about her, never showed up, I knew she wasn't." The light had faded, so it was hard for JT to see, but he thought Charlie looked upset. "I tried to ask you about it a couple times, but you never wanted to talk about Hailey so I let it go. It seemed like the kind of thing you'd do."

"What? Lie to everyone?"

"No. Stick by Hailey even though she dicked you over. So what did you say when you found out? You lay into her?"

JT rested his elbows on his knees. Hailey had been so frustrated over that tire. He'd have stopped to help anyone, but when he'd realized it was her he'd been happy. He knew how stupid it was, but he'd wanted to help her. Fact was, he couldn't say no to Hailey. Never had been able to.

Charlie must have read something in his face because he said, "Of all the women in all the world, how can you still be thinking about the one who cheated on you and then lied like this?"

"You have, like, charts on the women you've dated, don't you? Lists you can reorganize based on who's most likely to be a cheating recidivist. Is it in Excel or a database?"

"Shut up, JT. I'm just saying she never treated you right."

Which hadn't ever stopped him from thinking about Hailey before, so he wasn't sure why Charlie thought it would matter now.

CHARLIE LEFT a little later and JT went inside. Jack had moved from his chair to the recliner in the small family room off the kitchen. He had his feet up and was snoring loudly. Charlie had said that was where he'd been sleeping, so JT turned out the lights and grabbed his bag to head upstairs.

He stopped for a second on the landing halfway up the stairs and looked back down at the darkened living room. The white light from the streetlamp outside the house cut diagonally through the gap in the front curtains to illuminate his mom's face in the self-portrait hanging over the fireplace. It was one of the nudes she'd done the spring of his senior year of high school, when she'd been taking lessons from and sleeping with Trevor Meyers, the high-school art teacher. *His* high-school art teacher.

She'd rented a storefront on Main Street to show the series, but it had closed opening night when Jack threw a chair through the plate glass window. He and Melanie came so close to trading blows JT had told Charlie to get ready to dial 9-1-1, while he tried to figure out how he was going to manage his dad if he had to step in.

Later that night, when he and Charlie had been working through ideas for jumping Meyers and, teacher or not, showing him what they thought of him, Hailey had turned up crying. He took her out for a drive and that was when she told him she was pregnant. Two days later, after the meeting between their two families during which he wouldn't agree that Hailey should do a paternity test, his parents had kicked him out of the house.

He wondered what Jack thought about that painting over the mantel. What had his mom intended by putting it there? She'd never been discreet with her affairs, but surely his dad had minded. JT didn't think he'd ever understand their relationship, not if he had a million years and the Cliffs Notes.

The hallway was dark, all the doors closed, so he flicked on the sconce lights. Tomorrow he'd poke around and see what shape the house was in. For one, he'd find out why his dad was sleeping in a chair and not a bed. But for tonight he headed straight back to his old room at the far end of the hall.

He didn't know what he'd expected. He wouldn't have been surprised if his mom had stripped the place and put in exercise equipment, but it looked as if nothing had been touched since the night he'd sneaked out to propose to Hailey. He reached for the switch and the overhead light came on, illuminating the bunk bed, his desk, the bookcases... He couldn't believe it. The bulletin board was filled with a jumble of photos, ticket stubs from concerts and the picture the prom photographer had taken of him and Hailey. His high-school life was all right here as if he'd never left.

His telescope stood where it always had, pointed

toward the top half of his window. He took off the lens cover and then crouched to peer through the eyepiece, but the mountain ash in the backyard had grown and obscured his sight lines. He tried moving the stand but couldn't get a clear view. Trees had closed in everywhere.

His dad had given him the telescope when he was nine, but Jack hadn't ever understood exactly what JT liked about space.

Ironically, Jack had tried to interest him in the engineering aspects of space exploration, but at the time JT had really only cared about the stories. He'd been intending to grow up and work at McNulty's Garage with his dad, so becoming an engineer or even an astronaut hadn't interested him.

The stars and the stories he read about them—the myths that had been written about the constellations—that's what he'd liked. The constellations followed their seasonal patterns, showing up in the same spot, on time, every year.

He'd spent a lot of nights staring out at space. It was only later, after he'd left home and met Terrance, that he'd started to think about engineering as a career and space as more than a place full of cool stories.

JT ran a hand over the telescope and then closed the blinds. He stripped to his T-shirt and boxers, so exhausted he wanted to fall into bed.

The problem was, which bed? Confronted with the possibility of collapse if he chose the top bunk or claustrophobia in the bottom, JT wished for his king-size bed.

He climbed into the bottom bunk and switched off the lamp. The constellation map he'd made from stick-on stars glowed softly on the ceiling. He turned onto his side so he wouldn't be reminded of the way he'd felt when he was a kid, falling asleep every night so close to those stars that he could almost touch them.

The bunk bed was too small and the noises and smells of his old home unfamiliar to him, so it was a while before he finally drifted off to sleep. He dreamed that he landed on Mars in a huge ship that looked exactly like Hailey's Mustang, but had the RoboGen logo imprinted on the hood. When he got out, Hailey was already there, holding a baby. And both of them were waving to him.

CHAPTER FOUR

THE LIGHTS WERE ON in Sarah's house when Hailey eased the Mustang down the driveway and into the parking space next to the carriage house. She'd moved in here, renting from Sarah's parents, when she graduated from college. Olivia had been about to start kindergarten and Hailey had felt ready to strike out on her own, away from her parents' protectiveness.

Hailey sat in the car for a minute now, the scrapbook next to her. She recognized the polka-dot ribbon from a layout she'd done for Sarah's son, Simon, when he was born. Hailey had made her first scrapbook while she was waiting for Olivia to be born, because she hadn't been able to buy a baby book that didn't have lines and pages asking for details about the father. Over the years she'd made dozens of scrapbooks, and had also gotten Olivia started on the craft when she was still little.

Hailey fingered the ribbon, wondering what else she'd been teaching Olivia as she showed her how to use paper and glue to frame her memories. Scrapbooks were edited memories, the parts she wanted to save. Unwelcome details were obscured or hidden altogether. How often had she changed the truth as she made a scrapbook page? How much had Olivia learned from her?

Olivia had chosen to reach out to JT with a scrapbook. If only it hadn't been him Hailey would be happy to know that her daughter loved their family tradition enough to share it.

Hailey grabbed the book and went into the carriage house. The front room was dark, but down the hall she could see the lamp hanging low over the round kitchen table was on. After the encounter with JT, she didn't know if she could handle any more guilt, but she wouldn't avoid her daughter.

Olivia was leaning against the counter, her shoulders stiff and her face still tearstained. The rims of her eyes and her nose were red, her skin blotchy.

Hailey raised the scrapbook. "He didn't see this."

Olivia didn't react so Hailey put it on the table. She hadn't opened the book, and wouldn't. Olivia deserved respect for what had been meant as a private gift. Hailey knew if she left it here that her daughter would remove it at some point.

"I'm going out," Olivia said.

How was it possible that except for the evidence of tears, she was the same as always? Shouldn't there be some sign that her life had been turned upside down today? Maybe not, though. Maybe that kind of thing was carried not on a child's skin but in the parent's heart.

"Honey, I don't think that's a good idea. We've had a long day."

"I *need* to go out."

"Where are you going?"

"Why do you want to know?"

"Because you're fifteen and I'm your mother and you tell me where you're going when you leave the house."

"Fine. I'm going hang gliding. I'll be back by eleven." Olivia shrugged her sweatshirt on as if that settled things.

"I suppose I should have been more clear. You tell me the truth about where you're going when you leave the house."

Olivia's eyes filled with tears. "You lied to me for fifteen years."

"That's not the same."

"No. It's totally worse." Her daughter pushed off the counter, her hair swinging forward. "I'll be in my room. Since you can't trust me to go out without leaving an itinerary, I guess I'll never leave again."

"I do trust you, Olivia. I just want you to be safe."

"Whatever," Olivia retorted over her shoulder.

Hailey let her go, but it was hard. She and Olivia hardly ever fought. She'd almost hoped they might have weathered the teenage years without the traditional mother–daughter battles. But now, because of her, here they were.

Didn't Olivia know how much she loved her?

Know that everything Hailey had done and hadn't done was for her? Probably not. Probably kids never knew how their parents really felt about them—not until they became parents, anyway. And in truth, Hailey thought, it was better that way. No one could grow up normal knowing their every breath was counted and treasured and held so tightly in someone else's heart.

Hailey put in a load of laundry, but since she'd just done her weekly deep clean the day before, that was all the busy work she could come up with. The silence from Olivia's room was oppressive. Hailey kept looking at the door, wanting to knock and fix everything, but she knew she couldn't make this go away with a Band-Aid or a hug or even one good conversation. Her daughter needed time, but Hailey was so restless she worried she wouldn't have the self-control to give her that time.

"Olivia, I'm going to Sarah's," she called. There was no answer, but she hadn't expected one. She crossed the crushed-stone driveway and ran up the four slate stairs to Sarah's patio.

When she'd moved into the carriage house, Sarah's parents had still been living the main house. They'd moved to Florida the year Olivia was in second grade. Hailey had been concerned she might have to move, but then Sarah and her husband, Erik, had bought the main house and her life had been made immeasurably better with her best friend just across the driveway.

She knocked on the door and peered inside.

Through the glass she heard a muffled squeal from the family room and then Sarah's voice. "Lily, get off your brother. Right. Now."

Her friend backed into the kitchen, holding her mom glare on the activity in the family room until she appeared satisfied with what she saw. She smiled wearily at Hailey, waving for her to come in.

"Why does it seem like I'm a zookeeper more than a parent?" she asked. "What a day. Want a cup of tea?"

"How about a whiskey sour?"

Sarah's blue eyes revealed her concern as she took Hailey's hands. "Sweetie, you don't really want to drown your sorrows."

"Yes, I do. In fact, let's have a pitcher. With a whole jar of maraschino cherries."

"Well, if that's what you really want," Sarah said, but Hailey sighed and shook her head.

"It's a bad idea."

"Whiskey usually is. A lesser vice instead. A Coke? M&M's?" Sarah opened a narrow cupboard next to the stove and removed a folding step stool. After setting it down in front of the French door refrigerator she climbed onto the lowest step.

"I should have let you do this—you're tall enough to actually use my kitchen." She stretched to the back of the cupboard, her five-foot-two frame barely tall enough even with the stool. "I wish I'd put my foot down with Erik on this remodel. The whole room is too big for me—makes me feel like more of a midget than usual. Stupid man is convinced bigger is better."

Closing the cupboard, she hopped back down with a bag of plain M&M's. She ripped it open and poured the candy into a blue glass dish, which she shoved across the granite island toward Hailey. "Eat up. You need your strength."

"JT changed my tire," Hailey blurted, surprising herself as much as Sarah. It was almost worth the upset she was feeling to watch Sarah's face—her dear friend wanting to be supportive and having absolutely no idea how Hailey felt about seeing him.

"JT McNulty?"

Hailey nodded. Sarah popped three M&M's in her mouth.

"He said he's going to be here for a while, taking care of his dad," Hailey added, figuring she might as well drop the bomb so they could deal with the entire issue at once.

Sarah popped another handful of M&M's in her mouth. "I need water if we're not going to have whiskey. Are we having whiskey now?" she asked, her expression hopeful.

"I can't."

"Did you and JT talk?"

"All I did all day was talk. First Olivia. Then JT. JT again. And just now Olivia. Again. In all of these conversations, the other person was quite clear that I suck because I've been lying about Olivia's dad all these years."

Sarah started to reach for the M&M's, but dropped her hand. "This is bigger than chocolate, Hailey. What are you going to do?"

She slumped onto one of the red leather stools at the counter. "First, don't you want to tell me what a bad person I am?"

"Hailey, we've gone around on this before. This was your decision to make."

"But…"

"But I would have decided differently."

"I wanted to give her everything, you know?" Hailey felt drained and sad. Seeing JT again had been harder than she'd have expected. He'd seemed different than she'd remembered, and that made her doubt the clarity of her decision. Now, sitting in Sarah's bright, newly remodeled kitchen, she was irritated and tired and confused.

"You do give her everything. You work so hard and you love her so much. No kid ever had more reason to feel supported than Olivia."

"But I wanted her to have a dad, too. And JT said okay. He was with me when we told my folks…and his folks. He was right there."

Sarah came around the counter and pulled Hailey into a hug. Her friend was shorter than her, so sitting on the stool, she had to lean down. But it felt good to rest her head on Sarah's shoulder. The cool cotton of her sleeve soothed Hailey's cheek.

"Sweetie, the main question now is what are you going to do? Did Olivia flip out when she found out who her dad is?"

Hailey pulled back. "I didn't tell her that. I couldn't."

"You couldn't?"

"Sarah, Trevor Meyers is the principal of her school. She sees him every day. You know what he said about her."

Hailey still had nightmares every once in a while about Trevor. When she'd found out she was pregnant, she'd gone to him, hoping for…she didn't even know what. Support? Care? But he'd vowed he would never acknowledge the baby, never even come to see it.

That was when he'd told her she couldn't destroy his career and his family over this. She could sue him for paternity, but that wouldn't make him a father. It had brought home to her how much he'd enjoyed the control in their relationship. He'd known she wouldn't take him up on a dare, because she'd never resisted him before. He got off on that power. Still, she'd gone back to him one more time. After Olivia was born, Hailey had taken her picture-perfect little baby with her to his classroom when school was out, sure that not even Trevor would be able to resist the reality of Olivia. But he'd refused to look at the baby, had pulled out his checkbook.

She hadn't tried again. Olivia deserved better. Hailey had grown up in a safe, loving home where, if anything, she'd been overprotected. She couldn't imagine letting her daughter know her own father wouldn't even look at her. Or that her mother had been so hell-bent on breaking out of her sheltered life that the danger inherent in sneaking around with her teacher had been exciting instead of a deterrent. She'd never allowed herself to think about the man she was with or about his wife, she'd just let herself be seduced by the thrill and the risk. So she'd kept JT's lie going, and her daughter had someone to think about on Father's Day, as well as those damn birthday cards. And Hailey wasn't quite ready to agree with everyone that that had been a bad thing.

"Okay. I know. Trevor's an unforgivable bastard," Sarah said. "But what did you tell her?"

"That JT's not her dad. She went looking for him this morning. If I told her about Trevor, wouldn't she run right to him?" Hailey saw his face in her mind, his frozen expression as he stared at her across Olivia's stroller, then let the check flutter down on top of the baby. "Having sex with him was my mistake. She shouldn't have to pay for that."

"Where was JT? You didn't tell her all this in front of him?"

"I saw him later."

"The tire. Right. I love a man who's good with tools." Sarah slid onto the stool next to her and pulled the bowl of candy closer. She popped a few into her mouth, then closed her eyes. "Did you see them this morning? Him and Charlie? That is one good-looking family. Is that bad to say? It's probably a double sin if you have lustful thoughts during a funeral."

"Yeah, but it was Melanie. Her funeral probably

had a lust dispensation clause." Hailey watched her friend's face. There'd been something in Sarah's voice that made her wonder.... Not that she was actually lusting after either McNulty, but was that a trace of sadness or loneliness? "Funeral or no, though, are married ladies supposed to have lustful thoughts about unmarried men?"

"It's only a problem if we act on them." Sarah leaned her head on her hand. "What about you? Any lustful thoughts? Or actions?"

"Not at the funeral. But later? Unfortunately, yes."

"There were lustful thoughts? What was unfortunate about that?"

"Take your pick." Hailey held up her right hand and ticked the points off on her fingers. "One, the cosmos is against me. Two, JT all grown up is hot. Three, I'm a woman with a weakness for a nice back." She slumped over the counter. "Lots of things are unfortunate."

"Oh," Sarah said. "If only he'd gotten ugly, right?"

"If only."

Hailey wanted to go home, slip off her uncomfortable shoes, climb under the covers and never come out.

"So how is he? Besides hotter than you remember."

"Fine. Mad at me. It's strange he's going to take care of his dad. They didn't exactly part on good terms."

"It's been a long time. I'd imagine they want to put all that to rest."

"I guess I'll just hope they figure it out fast so he can go back to wherever he came from. Thanks for everything, Sarah."

Sarah pushed the bowl toward her. "You want to take these with you?"

She accepted the bowl more to try to seem normal than because she thought she'd eat any of the M&M's.

"Hailey?"

She turned back and waited.

"I'm on your side. Always have been. So I would never tell anyone about Trevor. But I think sometimes it might be better if you told."

Hailey felt a chill that made the hair on her arms stand up. "He said he wouldn't see her."

"But as long as it's a secret, she's going to wonder. Are you sure she's not old enough to handle it?"

"I sincerely doubt that fifteen is the right age to find out that your father has lived five miles away from you, is, in fact, the principal of your school, but has never wanted the slightest contact with you."

Sarah put her hands up in defeat. "When you put it that way…"

"I'm not putting it any way. That's the way it is."

They hugged again before Hailey headed back across the driveway to the carriage house. Inside, the place was quiet, which was one of the things Hailey liked most about her life with Olivia. But this wasn't the usual gentle quiet of their home, this was the quiet of a slasher movie scene when the less-than-bright-soon-to-be-dead coed walks downstairs alone.

Olivia's door was closed. Hailey stood outside and then tried the knob, thinking she'd just tuck Olivia in if she was already asleep. But the handle didn't turn. She'd never been locked out before.

Hailey leaned her head against the door and knocked softly. There was no answer. Maybe she was asleep. Maybe she hadn't heard. *Maybe she'd sneaked out.* No. Olivia wouldn't do that. Hailey stood for a moment, trying not to cry.

She was making the right choice. Olivia was curious about her father and Hailey would tell her someday…when she was old enough that the way he'd reacted wouldn't wound her so deeply. For now, though, Olivia was better off not knowing. Hailey needed to figure out a way to heal their broken trust.

CHAPTER FIVE

JT WAS STARTLED AWAKE the next morning by his cell phone. He'd been dreaming that he and Hailey were in the backseat of his rented Taurus, arguing about whether they'd be able to fit a baby seat in with them. He reached for the cell phone, happy to have something concrete to tether him to reality.

"Hello," he mumbled.

"You said you were going on vacation, not quitting."

JT was having trouble getting his brain going. "I didn't quit," he said, pretty sure he was talking to his business partner, Terrance Kurlow.

"I'm sorry, you *resigned.* Here, let me refresh your memory." Papers rustled on the other end and then Terrance read, "'Dear Terrance, I know you believe RoboGen needs to grow and pursue more wide-ranging projects, but I have reservations—' I love the part where you say 'wide-ranging' like you can't even bear to type 'space' because space is our goal and has been our goal all along. But let's see, yada, yada, here it is. 'I'm *resigning* effective—'"

"Stop, wait." JT swung his legs over the edge of

the bed and pushed his hair off his face. How had Terrance seen that? He hadn't actually resigned. Just because a person tested out some thoughts on scrap paper didn't mean… "I didn't give that letter to you."

"It was in a stack I got from Jeannie this morning. Did you write it?"

"Yes," JT admitted. He'd written it and then left it on his desk because he needed to think. It must have gotten mixed up with the rest of the paperwork he'd left for their assistant to give to Terrance.

"What for? You're taking a class in business correspondence and this is your exercise for the letter of resignation assignment?"

What for? He stood to pace across the room. How could he explain that the way Terrance had ramped up his push to take the next step—expanding RoboGen so they could pursue larger projects, specifically a part of a telescope for a Mars mission funded by NASA—had him freaked? RoboGen made component parts for larger robotics installations, mainly for scientific use so far, but there were a few commercial applications. Terrance had started the company as a spin-off from his graduate research in the robotics department at Carnegie Mellon University.

"You know why I wrote it. I'm not sure I'm ready to go ahead with the NASA bid or the expansion."

"What have we been doing all these years if we haven't been aiming for space?"

JT loved his work. The combination of the intricate intellectual tasks and the hands-on building involved in defining a problem and then designing the robotic solution was as satisfying to him as anything he'd ever done. But he'd never had the competitive edge he was going to need if they were to take the business bigger or compete for truly challenging projects.

"It's not just space. It's a human resources department and policies about vacation days. It's hiring more staff when we already have twelve people depending on us—my designs and your business plan—to keep them in paychecks, 401Ks and health insurance."

Most of all, he liked knowing he could handle just about any project RoboGen had the capacity to take on. It wasn't that he didn't think he could do more difficult work—it was that he wasn't convinced there was a reason to take the risk.

"I'll take care of the human resources and the 401Ks," Terrance said. "You only have to dream up the plans for us to build. That's your whole job."

"You make it sound like a no-brainer, Terrance. But you know how much can go wrong. No. The smart play is to stick with our niche where we know we're not going to fail."

No risk meant no risk of failure. JT was comfortable with that equation.

Terrance, however, lived and breathed risk. When they did a ropes course as a team-building exercise, he'd asked if he could be blindfolded just to take it up one more level. He'd been chafing at their inability to go after bigger projects. It had only gotten worse in the past two years, since their third partner, Glenn Jordan, had left RoboGen to start a competing firm.

"Fail? JT, it's a competitive bid. There's risk built into the process, but we can handle it."

"Look," JT blurted, "my mom died and I need a few days."

"Your..." Terrance paused, and when he spoke again his voice was gentle, as if he was afraid to spook JT. "Your mom? JT, you said you were going out of town. You didn't mention a funeral."

"I couldn't handle getting into the whole story. I'm sorry."

"God, JT. When will you... I'm sorry, man. If I'd known, I'd have come. I mean, your mom. I didn't even know... You never talked about her. Jeannie would have come. We all—"

"She wasn't that kind of mom."

Terrance was quiet. For a guy like him whose one big splurge after their first deal that was big enough to make a splurge possible went through had been a place at Seven Springs, where his family gathered every summer, JT's lack of contact with his parents had always been incomprehensible.

"I'm never going to understand you, am I?" Terrance said finally.

"I'm not complicated."

"And the Grand Canyon's a pothole."

"I need a few days."

There was a droning buzz and then a click. "Hear that?"

"Your shredder?"

"I might torch the pieces next." Terrance paused. "The way your brain works you could probably tape the shredded bits back together. Take some time and then come back. We can figure this out."

"Okay," JT said. They both knew that wasn't the end of the conversation, but for now Terrance backed off. JT was grateful.

"Call me."

"You got it."

He clicked the phone off and put it on the bed next to him. He hadn't slept well and Terrance's call had brought all of his worries crashing back. He heard a thump from downstairs and then his dad bellowed his name. Of course. Because being yelled at by his dad was exactly what he needed to make this day better fast. Wouldn't it be just his luck to get down there and find Hailey hanging around hoping for breakfast?

The prom photo caught his eye. He'd made her breakfast the morning after—they'd all stayed overnight at a friend's whose parents were out of town. He remembered that she liked scrambled eggs. Or at least she'd said she did.

HAILEY HATED IT when Olivia rolled her eyes. It wasn't the disrespect that got to her, although that was irritating. Hailey couldn't stand the thought that Olivia wasn't listening, wouldn't benefit from the things Hailey knew to be true.

She'd shut her own parents out and it had been a bad decision. She needed Olivia to keep talking to her so she wouldn't end up struggling with her issues alone. But now Olivia didn't trust her.

Their first day after the funeral hadn't gone so well. Olivia had been up and out before Hailey realized she'd gone, and then she hadn't answered her cell phone until close to three o'clock.

It was fine in theory to understand that kids need to make their own mistakes, but when you knew your kid had spent the previous day on a secret search for the father she'd never met, giving space to a fifteen-year-old headstrong daughter was a challenge.

Hailey crossed her legs and tried to steady herself as she sat on the white lace coverlet over the twin bed in Olivia's room. She should be standing; that would give her more authority. But she wanted a conversation, not a confrontation. Besides, the bedroom with its sloped ceiling was barely big enough for the two of them when they were calm. It certainly wouldn't be able to contain a battle.

Hailey and Olivia had designed the room together, painting branches and leaves on the walls and ceiling to create the effect of living in a tree house. It had always seemed like a safe retreat to Hailey before today.

"Rolling your eyes isn't helping convince me you're responsible."

"I don't know why I have to convince you I'm responsible. When have I done anything that makes you think I'm not?"

Skipping school to meet up with the man she thought was her dad was one good example. But mentioning it would almost certainly lead them further into an argument.

"Okay, you're right. I have always been able to count on you," Hailey said. "My point is that now that it's summer and you're home alone while I'm at work, we need procedures. I want you to call me at work in the morning before you leave the house, and I want you to leave your phone on and answer it if I call."

"You called eight times before lunch."

"I wouldn't have called eight times if you'd answered once!"

Olivia crossed her arms and smiled that satisfied little smile that meant she knew she'd pushed Hailey into yelling when she didn't want to. "Fine. Whatever," she said.

Calm, Hailey thought. *Don't kill her. Keep her talking.*

"When I saw you yesterday, it seemed as if you knew Mr. McNulty. Like maybe yesterday wasn't the first time you met him."

Olivia was quiet, which was all the answer Hailey needed. If there'd been reason to protest, her daughter wouldn't have missed it.

"So," Hailey continued, "I feel like you've been sneaking around. And I want to know where you are and what you're doing."

"I wasn't doing anything wrong. I thought he was my grandfather."

"How did you meet him?"

"Why does it matter? He's not going to want to talk to me ever again."

"It matters because I need to know how long you've been lying to me."

As soon as Hailey said it she wished she could pull the words back into her mouth, like reeling in a fishing line. The look Olivia gave her was so full of disgust that she found herself wishing for a good old-school eye roll instead.

"A lot less than fifteen years," Olivia said, and then she was off the bed and out the door faster than you could say "my mother is a lying hypocrite."

Nobody was going to be asking Hailey to write the parents' column for the *Statlerville Journal* anytime soon. Which was ironic because until all this happened, she'd thought she was doing all right.

She pressed a hand to her abdomen and forced herself to straighten up, doing a few shoulder rolls to release tension.

She wondered what Mr. McNulty thought. Had JT told him the truth? Would he want to stay in touch with Olivia or would he cut her off again? Most of what Hailey knew about Jack McNulty was gossip she'd gotten from her mother, or stories she'd heard from JT. He'd never shown any interest in Olivia before. Hailey had actually invited him and his wife to Olivia's baptism and her first birthday party, but they hadn't responded, and as far as she knew they'd never been in touch. But her daughter had looked distressed that he might not want to talk to her again. And Hailey had seen them hug yesterday. She'd guessed that their relationship was recent, but it seemed real, and it worried her because it was entirely out of her control.

BEFORE HE'D BEEN HOME twenty-four hours, JT had developed a maddening symptom of what he was sure was sudden onset insanity. He was hearing voices. Scratch that. He was hearing a voice, inside his head. That it was his own voice should have made it okay, but instead made it all the more irritating.

It had started when his dad took a swing at him the first morning just because he got the wheelchair jammed in the doorway of the downstairs bathroom. How was he supposed to know the damn doorway was too narrow? His dad couldn't have spoken up before JT wedged it in there? And why the hell hadn't someone widened the doorway sometime in the six months since his dad's legs had been injured in the accident at the garage?

Whatever the chain of blame, when Jack smacked him while JT was bent awkwardly forward, trying to unhook the footrest from the door hinge, he heard the voice for the first time. It suggested a swift and immediate exit from Statlerville. It had taken a second to recover from the surprise of his dad's hand connecting in a familiar, semi-painful way with the back of his head.

"Dad!" he yelled as he straightened quickly, stepping out of range. "Don't hit me."

"Don't jam me into spaces where the damn chair won't fit."

"How about a heads-up next time? You didn't know it wouldn't fit?"

"I didn't know you were a moron. Thought you'd see the space is too small."

JT gave the chair a wrench and it jerked backward, ramming him in the stomach. *That hurt.* He scrambled around, practically climbing over his dad to get in front of him.

"Look. Here's the deal. I'm not a kid anymore. You don't get to hit me. You don't get to call me names."

"You act like a moron, I'll call you a moron."

"You call me a moron and I'll stick you in that doorway nice and tight and be back at the airport on my way to Pittsburgh before you can say 'Jack McNulty is a monumental jackass.'"

Jack glared at him, but he didn't bite back. Which made JT nervous. He'd never in his life won an argument with his dad and didn't quite know what to do now that he had.

"That's what you want? To get out of here as fast as you can?"

"I want to help you get stuff sorted out."

Jack didn't answer him.

JT gestured toward the bathroom. "Do you, um, need help? With anything?"

If his dad said he needed help peeing JT was calling Charlie and invoking whatever big-brother privilege he needed.

Jack set the brakes on the wheelchair and put his hands on the armrests. "Help me up."

JT folded the footrests out of the way, moved next to his dad and helped him lever himself upright. Then he watched as Jack clutched the door frame and shuffled forward. He shifted his grip to the bathroom wall and moved his legs with painful slowness. Right about the time JT thought he couldn't watch anymore and was going to offer to help no matter if it scarred him for life, Jack reached behind him and slammed the door shut.

Nothing wrong with his upper-body strength, was there?

CHARLIE CAME BY as promised that evening and the three of them took paper plates full of the neighbors' donated food out on the porch.

"The wheelchair doesn't fit in the bathroom," JT said before he took a bite of the baked ziti he'd heated up in the microwave.

Charlie stopped picking the onions out of his salad to glance with mild interest at his dad, as if expecting Jack to respond.

"I'm talking to you, Charlie," JT said. "How come nothing's fixed up here for him? He's been in that chair six months. Why didn't you or Mom get someone to at least put up some grab bars?"

"I'm not sitting here if the two of you are going to talk around me all night again," Jack growled.

"I asked you fifteen times why you hadn't been to physical therapy and you didn't answer me once," JT said in frustration.

"I'm not doing physical therapy," Jack snapped. "Consider yourself answered."

"You see why I stopped asking you."

"He refused therapy," Charlie confirmed. "And she refused to get someone in to remodel. It was a stalemate."

"It was none of your business," Jack said. "Still isn't."

JT put his plate down next to him. The ziti had probably been barely decent even when it was fresh. The reheated version wasn't doing anything for him. What he wanted was to be home in his house in Pittsburgh, with a burger on the grill followed by a pickup game of Ultimate in the park. But he wasn't there, he was here, and he needed to figure out something between him and his dad. This time when he left Statlerville he wanted it to be on his own terms, whatever they might be.

"What about the garage? How have you been handling work?" he asked.

"Garage is closed," Jack said bluntly. "I quit."

"What?" JT was floored. His dad loved McNulty's Garage. JT and Charlie had grown up on the family story of Jack starting the place when he was fresh out of high school, and all the up-by-your-bootstraps lore that had gone with it. They'd lived in the tiny apartment behind the garage for the first two years of JT's life. His parents had only bought a house when Charlie came along.

The garage had grown into a very successful business, funding their tuition at St. Pete's, the big house on Cedar, membership at the country club and all of his mother's forays into art and drama. McNulty's was as much of a home to his dad as anywhere else, and it had been the only place he and his dad ever felt totally comfortable with each other.

"Once I did my legs I knew I wasn't going back to work so I shut the place down."

"But you…your legs…it's not supposed to be permanent, Dad." JT had discussed this with Charlie back when the accident with the lift happened. "You were supposed to do therapy and then you were supposed to be up and around again."

Jack focused pointedly on the yard. *Right. No therapy.*

"What about Leon and the other guys? Couldn't they have kept it going until you came back?" JT turned to his brother. "How did you let this happen? Couldn't you get someone to run it while he rehabbed?"

"I'm not *rehabbing!*"

Jack spoke at the same time that Charlie said, "Why do you think he'd have let me help him?"

"The place is closed, JT. End of story."

Which explained why none of those guys who'd worked there forever had been at his mom's funeral. If Jack had yanked the rug out from under them, they were probably pissed.

"Dad, I'm trying to understand. You loved that place…"

"Look, son, you don't have to understand everything. You're here to babysit me, and that's all you need to worry about."

"Charlie?" JT said.

"What?"

"Yeah," Jack said, "what?"

There was a blatant challenge in his father's eyes. Ever since his dad had ordered him to stay he'd been after something. He wouldn't come right out and ask for whatever it was, so he was poking and prodding JT, trying to drive him toward the end game. JT was in no mood to be herded.

When JT was a kid his refusal to compete at sports or school or anything had infuriated his father. Jack lived for the thrill of victory.

The wounds his parents had inflicted on each other and on him and Charlie in the name of love—not to mention Hailey's rejection—had proved to JT that it didn't pay to let anything matter.

JT was nervous about what his father might want from him now. He'd spent a lot of time trying to let go of his parents. And the more time he spent with his dad, the more he realized it was harder than ever to understand the man. So he should treat this like a job. He'd help get Jack situated, get him started on physical therapy, make some improvements to the house and then he'd go.

When he got back to Pittsburgh his old life would be waiting for him, and all this confusing business of being a son and a fake father and an ex-boyfriend would fade away again. It had to because he felt like he was going crazy.

"Here's what. After we're finished eating, Charlie's going to help me move a bed into the dining room. No more sleeping in the chair. Tomorrow you and I are going to the hardware store and we're getting grab bars and supplies to make a ramp for the porch. After that, you're going to start therapy."

Charlie blinked. Then he moved his plate and bottle carefully to the other side of his chair as if to protect them from the outburst he was obviously expecting.

JT's pulse was racing as he watched his dad. Ultimatums in the McNulty family came from Jack, they weren't directed toward him.

"Fine," Jack said. "But no therapy."

He wheeled his chair back into the kitchen, letting the door slam behind him.

"That went well," Charlie said quietly.

"At least he only slammed the door," JT answered.

"No, I meant it sincerely." His brother picked up his plate again. "What did you do to him? He actually agreed to something."

"I don't know. I think he wants something from me. He tried to hit me this morning and I told him to back off and he did."

"I'm keeping an eye on you. One more miracle and I'm applying to the diocese to have you sainted."

"Don't I need to be dead to be a saint?"

"With you and Dad living together it's probably just a matter of time." Charlie finished the last bite of his casserole. "You tell him about the kid yet?"

"Not yet. He's so closed down. I haven't figured out what to say."

"What if she shows up?"

JACK KEPT HIS HANDS to himself and the moron comments to a minimum as he watched JT and Charlie wrestle the dining-room table out to the garage and then move the guest-room bed downstairs.

Charlie headed out soon after they finished, and JT knocked on the frame of the dining-room door. "You okay?"

His dad was already in the bed, lying flat with his hands crossed behind his head. "Did you take any calls for me today?" he asked.

"No. Were you expecting someone?"

Jack nodded. "I was." He pulled one arm out from behind his head and studied his watch. "Tomorrow is Wednesday, right?"

JT nodded and his dad seemed to come to some decision. He pulled his covers up and pointed to the hall. "Turn out that light before you go upstairs."

JT did as he was told. He was crossing the living room when his dad called, "The bed is nice, son."

JT shook his head. Jack actually thanking him for anything would probably qualify as one of the signs of the apocalypse. "You're welcome," he called back.

CHAPTER SIX

"WE'RE DOING TWO MORE reps and then you can take a break."

"Two more reps might kill me, Hailey," Rita muttered even as she tightened her thigh and hip muscles to begin the lifts.

Hailey watched her carefully, knowing the tiny, retired professor was prone to trying to overdo things—she was impatient to be finished with her therapy after a hip replacement.

On Wednesdays Hailey opened Viva Rehab Center. Cynthia, her partner, had an in-home patient that she saw early and Debby, their receptionist, was taking a financial accounting class at the junior college.

Hailey liked the quiet on Wednesday mornings. Before her first appointment, she ran the vacuum and wiped down the equipment even though she knew the cleaning crew had done all that the night before. She liked making order in this space that she'd helped design and grow. Viva was her entire security, and checking it over once a week made her feel in control.

Hailey put a hand on Rita's knee to remind her to watch her extension.

And she did. Hailey loved patients like Rita, Viva's success stories.

Cynthia had approached her about opening a practice together when Hailey was in the last year of her college program. They'd been through elementary school and then high school together, but while Hailey delayed college for a few years, Cynthia had gotten her degree and gone to work for a center just across the New Jersey border. She'd gotten frustrated by the conflict she felt between the patients and the center's national-chain-brand owners and thought she and Hailey could do a better job.

It had been Hailey's inspiration to design Viva with a retro look and homey touches like the café curtains and a jukebox that played oldies to cater to their mainly geriatric clientele. Large framed prints showing black-and-white scenes from 1940s and 1950s movies completed the nostalgic atmosphere. Everything from the paint colors to the texture of the carpet was calibrated to create a calm, clear energy.

When Rita finished her last set, Hailey brought her a towel and watched as she headed slowly, but with more confidence than last week, for the locker rooms. That was Hailey's reward right there. Watching one of her clients gain their balance or mobility or independence. She'd gotten into physical therapy because she wanted to help people.

Her clients took the bad hands they were dealt, and with her assistance, many of them changed the game.

The big clock over the front door showed her she had ten minutes before her next client was due. Good thing, because she'd missed at least two phone calls while she was with Rita. Maybe the rehab center should hire Olivia to work the reception desk on Wednesdays for the summer, she thought. It would keep her daughter out of mischief and give Hailey and her something to talk about.

WHEN JT CAME DOWNSTAIRS, his dad was still in bed. JT knocked on the dining-room door and said he was going for a run. Jack didn't answer, so he eased the door open. His father was lying under the covers, staring at the ceiling.

"You want me to help you get up before I go?"

"I don't need your help."

"Fine," JT said.

"Bring me the phone, would you?"

JT got the phone from its base in the kitchen and brought it to his dad while he added *cell phone* to his mental shopping list.

Jack looked up at him impatiently. "You going to stand there like a mor—like a lump, or are you going to help me up?"

JT had helped him get dressed the day before, so he knew better what to expect, but it was still hard. Neither of his parents had been physically affectionate toward him and Charlie, so he had little experience being this close to his dad. When Jack held his shoulder for stability, the combination of the strength in his grip and the trembling instability of his legs was unsettling. JT pulled his dad's pants up carefully and then brought the wheelchair over while Jack tucked his shirt in.

"I get why you don't want to have a nurse," JT said. He wouldn't have wanted to rely on a stranger for that kind of help, either. "But you have to try rehab or you're going to get worse."

"Enjoy your run."

JT backed toward the door. "I won't be more than half an hour."

Jack ignored him.

JT wasn't entirely sure it was a good idea to leave him alone. If Jack fell there was no way he could get back into the chair. But JT needed to get some exercise, clear his head. He and his dad were going to kill each other if they spent twenty-four hours a day together.

He was going to have to find someone to come in and sit with Jack a little bit every day. That would give JT time to work on the stuff he and Terrance had to hash out, and if he was lucky he could find a pick-up Ultimate game somewhere to keep him sane. And he knew there were more adaptations they could make to the house to make things easier. For now, he jumped down the front steps and started out at a fast pace, hoping to work off some of his restlessness and worry. He'd take half an hour, no more, and he wanted to use it hard.

JT JOGGED HOME to cool down, enjoying his adrenaline high. The exercise had been just what he needed to clear his mind and get him back in a place where he could deal with his dad.

His dad, who was on his front porch talking to a girl with a green backpack and red sneakers. JT had a sinking feeling he knew exactly who that girl was.

The two of them stopped talking when his foot hit the bottom step. Jack gave him the look that was rapidly becoming familiar, the one that made JT want to examine his conscience for occasions when he'd broken the Honor Thy Father commandment. The girl was tall and thin with long, dark-brown hair, dressed in jeans and a T-shirt that showed a vampire playing a video game over the words, "Vampires have no life." When JT met her eyes, she crossed her arms in front of her chest and let her hair fall forward across her face, but he recognized her, anyway. It was the girl from the funeral, just as he'd guessed. Hailey's kid.

Now that he knew, yeah, he saw a resemblance. Olivia had the same dark eyes and wide forehead, the same deep-brown hair. But where Hailey had been practically a carbon copy of her mom, Olivia had her own unique look. Not her own, though, JT corrected himself. Some influence from her father. Whoever he might be.

"Hi," he said, careful to keep his tone neutral.

"This is Olivia," Jack said. "I don't think you've met."

"Hi," he repeated. Tomorrow he was installing a

fire alarm on the porch so the next time a situation like this came up he could pull it and…*his dad was talking.*

"What?" he asked.

"I said Olivia and I got to know each other this spring, right after my accident." Jack was so cool he might have been introducing business colleagues on the veranda at the country club. JT wondered if it would upset his not-daughter if her not-father punched her not-grandfather in the nose.

"Does your mom know you're here?" he blurted.

He wouldn't have thought it was possible for the girl to hunch any further, but she did, rounding her shoulders and dropping her head. His dad glared at him, but it was unnecessary. JT hadn't meant to make her upset, he just didn't know what to do.

"Mr. McNulty called me," she said. And then she whispered out of the side of her mouth to Jack, "You said he was gone out."

"He said he was going running. I figured he'd go farther than around the block."

"Hey," JT protested.

They looked at him.

"I was gone twenty-seven minutes."

"Twenty-seven?" Jack said skeptically.

JT lifted his arm to show them his watch. "This is an atomic watch, guaranteed to be correct. It recalibrates every night against the U.S. atomic clock in Fort Collins." The girl and his dad were both giving him that look he knew meant he'd been too geeky for normal people. "I didn't want to leave you alone," he said. "No need to make fun when I was only thinking of you."

"I don't need a babysitter," Jack snapped.

"I should go," the girl said quietly.

"You remember what I said," Jack told her. "It's all going to be okay." And then he patted her arm.

JT watched, dumbfounded. His dad didn't pat people. He hardly even acknowledged anyone else's feelings, let alone tried to soothe them. And yet there he was, his large, red-knuckled workman's hand rough and awkward against the kid's slim forearm. Even stranger, Olivia didn't seem fazed by it. She touched Jack's hand in response, almost as if this were a common occurrence, as if the two of them exchanged physical affection like this all the time.

"Good luck," she said. She raised her head and, with the first show of spunk JT had seen from her, said, "That's a nice watch."

"That's a nice shirt," he replied. She had Hailey's smile.

Jack chuckled as she left. "Okay, ready to go?"

"What? Where?"

"Physical therapy, remember?" Jack said, and while he didn't add "moron," it was definitely implied.

JT put a hand behind him to find the porch banister, and leaned on it. He felt as if he hadn't had a coherent thought since he'd walked into the service the other day. Or even before that, since Charlie called and gave him the news. His dad kept making these pronouncements and JT was constantly playing catch-up.

"We have to talk about some stuff first," he said.

"No we don't."

"Dad, we do. Olivia. I… We need to talk about Olivia."

Jack's gaze sharpened. "You bet we need to talk about Olivia. But not now. Now we need to get me signed up for physical therapy. You're the one who put it on the to-do list."

"Since when do you do anything I say," JT muttered.

"Since it suits me," Jack replied. "Now help me down the stairs. You drive. I'll tell you where we're going."

"I need to change."

Jack looked him up and down. "I'll wait here while you shower. Don't take too long, though. I haven't had breakfast yet."

"Dad—"

"Listen, we're in the car in fifteen minutes or I'm not going ever. It's a one-time offer, just like they have on TV."

"That's ridiculous. You're the one who's going to benefit from therapy. You wouldn't stay in that wheelchair to spite me."

Jack folded his arms. "Watch me."

The pose and the threat were both familiar from his childhood. The fifteenth-anniversary trip to Italy his parents had forfeited over an argument about whether Jack should pack two suits or three. The many times a customer had tried in vain to protest a bill at the garage. The last argument JT had had with his folks. He'd waited fifteen years for Jack to back down that time.

"I'll be ready in five minutes," he said.

THEY TOOK THE RENTED Taurus because it was easier to fit the wheelchair in the back than in his dad's MG. JT remembered how Hailey had looked sitting in the backseat, obviously flustered and trying her best to be dignified with that ridiculous story about her client. He still hadn't figured out what she'd really been doing back there. He wasn't about to admit to himself or anyone else exactly how much time he'd spent thinking about it.

Jack directed him to a low building on the edge of the main shopping district downtown. JT thought it had been an insurance agency when he was a kid, but now the sign out front read Viva Rehabilitation and Physical Therapy.

He pushed the button for the automatic doors and waited while his dad went through ahead of him. The interior was spooky at first, like a set for a World War II movie about "the folks back home." The jukebox in the corner was even playing what he was pretty sure was a Glenn Miller song. He lagged a few steps behind his dad while he checked the place out, so he didn't see her until she'd already noticed them. *Hailey.*

Thank you so much, Dad.

If he were ever going to discover a latent super

power, now was the time. He wouldn't even be choosy about which one—invisibility, evaporation, flying, hell, he'd take the power to smite people with lightning bolts—the back of Jack's head was looking mighty tempting right now. Smiting his dad wouldn't solve his problem, but it would feel good and plus he could use the smiting as a diversion while he escaped.

She was behind the computer at the reception desk, her thick brown hair pulled back and caught in a tortoiseshell clip, with long, wavy strands hanging down to frame her face. She was wearing a white blouse with a black-and-white silk scarf knotted low in the open neck, and black pants. She looked put together. Even her black climbing-style shoes were stylish.

"JT," she said. "Mr. McNulty."

No inflection. Nothing. As if they'd never met or meant anything to each other. As if she hadn't been telling people for fifteen years that they shared a child. Well, what else should he expect? It wasn't as if they really shared a child. Or anything else, for that matter.

"Dad?" he said quietly, hoping for some information about why they were here.

Jack ignored him and nodded at Hailey.

Then the two of them were staring at JT. Which made no sense, because he was the person in the room with the least information about what the hell was going on.

"Dad," he said, knowing he sounded and probably looked about six years old. That made him even more angry at his father for putting him in this position. "Why are we here?"

Hailey blushed, the warmth spreading up her neck into her cheeks. *What* were *they doing here?*

She couldn't imagine what they wanted, but then she remembered that JT had said he was going to tell his father about Olivia. Surely they hadn't come here, to her business, to talk about that? Hailey checked her watch. Mr. Turner had ten more minutes in the whirlpool, but then she'd need to help him out.

"We're short-staffed here today and I really need to—"

"I'm here to start physical therapy," Mr. McNulty said.

She tried to get a view of the calendar, but couldn't see the names. Cynthia wouldn't have taken him on as a patient without telling her, would she? "So," Hailey said, squinting and scanning the list frantically, unable to locate his name on the appointment sheet, "what time was your appointment?"

"I need to make one," Mr. McNulty stated. "With you."

"What?" JT asked.

His dad crossed his arms. "You said, 'Tomorrow you're staring therapy.' So get me started."

"Dad. Shut it." JT smiled weakly at Hailey, appearing incredibly uncomfortable. "I'm sorry. I didn't know you worked here or we wouldn't have come."

"*I* knew she worked here and it's *exactly* why we came."

Hailey watched JT try to navigate this conversation, and felt bad for him. He was absolutely out of his depth, but just as cute as he had been in high school, in his gray-and-black ringer tee and long black shorts. His hair was damp, as if he'd just showered. She could tell he was trying to support his dad, but wondered if he needed help himself. From where she was sitting Jack seemed to have the upper hand. In fact, she was reminded quite a bit of her last confrontation with Olivia.

"Mr. McNulty, wouldn't you prefer to work with my partner, Cynthia Dansel?"

"Cynthia is a physical therapist?" JT blurted. "She beat me up in first grade. Never seemed like the caring and sharing type."

"Obviously I can't work with someone who beat up my son," Jack said, and again Hailey was reminded of Olivia in one of her one-upmanship moods. "So it's got to be you."

"Hailey!" Mr. Turner's low voice came from the whirlpool room.

"Please excuse me for a moment. I have a patient," Hailey said.

When she got back to the desk, she was surprised to find JT there by himself. He looked exasperated and confused and totally hot. His legs were lean but muscular, his calves sculpted and his thighs…well, she was able to stop staring, but only with effort, and it was much harder than it should have been.

She sat in Debby's chair, glad to have the counter between them. She dealt with bodies all day, but not like JT's. He was distracting and confusing and almost enough to make her forget that his dad…

"What in the world is your dad thinking?" she asked.

"I don't have the faintest clue. But your daughter was at the house this morning, so I'm pretty sure it has something to do with her."

"Why was she there? You said you were going to tell him about Olivia. Didn't you tell him? Where did he go, anyway?"

"I haven't told him yet," JT admitted. "He's waiting outside." JT was standing in the shadow thrown by a post in the entryway, with the light coming over his shoulder. His eyes were a deeper, darker blue than she remembered.

Blue eyes or not, she needed to focus. "Well, now we have a problem."

"The problem happened when you lied to all these people. Me taking an extra three days to talk to my dad did not cause the problem." She watched the rapid rise and fall of his chest and knew he was angry but trying not to show it.

He was right, and he had every reason to be mad at her. But Olivia and Jack had made some kind of connection and it seemed to matter to them. Which was a surprise, because Jack McNulty had had years to be in Olivia's life and he'd never shown up. But now, with JT home and the truth almost out in the open, when it wasn't possible anymore, all of a sudden there he was. It made Hailey feel worse than she already did.

"Well, I can't work with him."

JT straightened. "Oh no. You have to work with him."

"What?"

"He needs therapy. He wouldn't even talk about it for six months and now he's ready to start? You can't not do it."

"Why, because I owe you?"

JT snorted and shook his head. "No." He walked to the door of the treatment room and turned his back. She could tell how carefully he was controlling his voice when he spoke. "If there was any way he'd work with someone else, believe me, Hailey, I'd take him somewhere else."

JT came back and stood in front of her, placing his hands on the counter as if trying to calm down. There was the same worry and pain on his face that she saw in so many of the people who brought family members in for care. "He says if you won't work with him then he's not doing therapy. Which from someone else might be an empty threat, but from him is a statement of fact. Hailey, if you could see him, he can barely manage. The way he's living, it's not okay. Especially not if he could get better."

This was so wrong, in so many ways. And likely to get worse. But Hailey had gone into PT to help people. Plus, whether JT would admit it or not, she did owe him.

Maybe if she helped his dad that would in some small way help to relieve her guilt.

"You will tell him about Olivia, though?" she said. "Because he might not want to...if he knows."

"I'll tell him. But if it doesn't change his mind, you'll do it?"

"We'll set up a consultation and take it from there, okay?"

She was watching him, so she saw when he took in a deep breath. Saw his shoulders pull back and the T-shirt stretch tight across his shoulders. Her eyes traced the muscles of his chest, and right there in her own reception area, she had thoughts of a most unprofessional nature about getting him out of his ringer tee to run her hands across what she knew was a well-defined set of abs.

She felt him watching her and, when their eyes met, knew he'd followed the detour her eyes had taken and that he knew she had appreciated the journey. She almost smiled. Funny that they'd still have that quick connection.

"Sorry."

He shrugged, not interested in her perusal or her apology. "Old habits. Doesn't mean anything."

Perhaps not to you, she thought. She focused on the desk, pulling out an appointment card, glad he couldn't see her face.

"Maybe after the consult he'll accept a referral to someone else."

"Okay," JT said. "I'll hope for that."

The door opened and she expected to see Jack.

But it was Cynthia's next appointment, Mrs. Perkins, the retired third-grade teacher and their least favorite patient. She had the sourest face Hailey had ever seen on a real person. The face, coupled with her piercing voice, had made third grade hell for Hailey's entire generation. Mrs. Perkins also had a demanding manner and a serious complex about being ignored.

"I'm ready for my appointment," she announced as soon as she crossed the threshold.

"Mrs. Perkins, I'm sorry, but your appointment is at ten forty-five. If you'll have a seat, Cynthia will be with you at that time." She would if she knew what was good for her anyway.

"I suggest you check the book again," Mrs. Perkins said. "Who's this young man? You're not selling memberships, are you? Viva is a health center, not a gymnasium."

JT hadn't taken his eyes off Mrs. Perkins since she'd walked in. The older woman didn't recognize him, but judging by the dumbstruck expression on his face, he knew exactly who she was.

"Mrs. Perkins, you remember JT McNulty, don't you?"

"Jonathon McNulty, Junior," Mrs. Perkins said. "The only boy who ever got suspended from my third grade twice before Christmas. You left town. Were you incarcerated?"

Hailey choked as JT straightened with a guilty expression. "Incarcerated? No, ma'am. I, uh, went to college."

"Hmph. Well, I'm not surprised you've come home with your tail between your legs. Gambling debts, no doubt."

JT gaped at her as Hailey put a hand to her mouth to hide her smile. Cynthia came in the side door and said, "Mrs. Perkins, I'm ready when you are." She mouthed, "I'm sorry" and pointed to her watch as she put a hand under Mrs. Perkins elbow to guide her into the treatment area.

It took a second for JT to recover. "My company was on the cover of *Science* magazine last year," he said. Mrs. Perkins ignored him.

"Didn't she used to be a lot taller?" he asked.

"Your company was in *Science* magazine?"

Her surprise must have been obvious, because his head jerked back, as if she'd insulted him. "RoboGen. We design robotics."

"Robotics? Really? I had no idea. You never… I mean, in school…you didn't seem like you paid much attention."

"I guess neither of us knew each other very well," he said. Their eyes met and she wondered what else she didn't know about him.

"Listen, Hailey, I know you don't want to work with my dad, but can we just make the appointment and I'll see what I can do about talking him into going somewhere else?"

Of course. This was business for him. Why would she expect anything else? The next day was booked tight, but she could probably have Rita work with Cynthia this once. "Can you bring him by at ten tomorrow?"

"Um, he kind of wants to do it at our house."

"I'd rather see him here."

"He…" JT paused, embarrassed. "He said this place is for old people." He glanced around. "I mean, I can see it's great. The way you've made it all retro and everything. But for him, I think maybe the pictures or the music were too much."

"I'll see him at home. Once. That's it."

JT smiled. It wasn't his usual full-on smile with the eye crinkles and the nose wrinkle. It was a little sad, a little…regretful. "Thanks. I want him to get better."

"I'm sure it's possible. We can do a lot for people if they're willing to work."

JT nodded as he headed for the front door.

Hailey watched him go, his walk full of self-confidence. How else had he changed, she wondered, in the years he'd been gone? Remembering the way he'd dismissed her attempt at connection… old habits…she didn't expect she'd have much chance to find out even if she did take Jack on as a client.

JT STOPPED FOR TAKEOUT from the Main Street Diner. His dad didn't say anything in the car and JT didn't trust himself to speak, either. He was seriously pissed about that ambush. At Jack and himself. Had he known Hailey was a physical therapist? He couldn't remember. But he sure as hell knew his dad was a master manipulator. JT needed to bone up on his old McNulty family survival skills. Foremost among them was the saying, "If it looks too easy, it is too easy."

The part he still couldn't figure out was why Hailey? Why would Jack twist them all around just to be sure he worked with Hailey? It had to be the kid, JT knew, especially considering Jack's reassurance to her that everything would be okay, right before he'd brought up the therapy. JT hoped like hell his dad wasn't matchmaking because as much as he still found Hailey attractive, he didn't trust her.

When they got back to the house, JT carried the cardboard tray full of lunch into the kitchen, then went back to help Jack out of the car and carry the wheelchair up the steps.

His dad had said he was hungry earlier, so JT was surprised when he went straight through the kitchen and into his office. The last thing JT wanted to do was follow him down there and tell him about Olivia. But the longer he let it go, the worse it was going to be.

He had to smile at that irony. He probably could have waited until after lunch. A couple hours wouldn't make that much difference after fifteen years. On the other hand, who knew what his dad was up to now? In the space of one morning he'd certainly messed with enough people. JT should get in there and get this done.

He knocked and stood in his dad's open door. Each of the three floors of the house had a circular turret room. This one had floor-to-ceiling windows on the outside walls and floor-to-ceiling bookcases on the inside one. The dark walnut woodwork and the heavy furnishings gave the room a somber air.

JT had never been comfortable in here. He propped one shoulder on the door frame and waited.

"What?" Jack said, without looking up from the book in his lap.

"We were going to talk about Olivia."

"So talk."

Jack's face was partially obscured by shadows thrown by the sunlight coming through the lilac bushes outside the window. JT couldn't tell what his dad was feeling or what he might know.

"She seems like a nice kid."

"Is that really what you think we need to talk about?"

JT's shoulders jerked. He hadn't realized how tense he was.

"I'm sorry that you and she…that you met or…" He wasn't making sense. "Dad, I'm sorry, but she's not my kid."

Jack slammed the book he'd been pretending to read closed. "She told me that this morning. When did you find out?"

"I knew all along."

"Why in the hell would you lie? Why would you throw your life away over some girl who cheated on you?"

"I didn't throw my life away."

"You threw our family away."

JT took two steps forward, fighting a practically overwhelming desire to punch his dad. "You told me to get out and stay out."

Jack banged his closed fist on the desk. "No.

First your mother and I begged you, JT. We begged you to at least ask for a paternity test. But you stood there and you lied right to our faces, swore up and down that child was yours. Why?"

"You didn't beg me. I begged you. I came to you. I wanted to marry Hailey, but I wanted to convince her and her family. But Mom said if I was going to believe Hailey, and if I wouldn't go along with your plan for a paternity test and some big court battle, than I should just get out. She said I had to choose between you guys and Hailey, and you stood right next to her and backed her up."

"You were seventeen! Hadn't been to college. Didn't even have your high school diploma in your hand. And you wanted us to hand over your college fund so you could marry some girl? We'd have been bad parents if we agreed to that."

JT took a deep breath, trying to calm down. He realized with a start that there were three pictures on his dad's desk—of him, Charlie and Olivia. JT gestured toward the group. "How long ago did you meet her?"

"About nine months. She came to the garage. Pretended she wanted a job, but I knew who she was. I told your mom and she said I should ignore her if she came back." Jack's mouth twisted. "Your mom never met her. Wouldn't let her come to the house."

He stopped and JT waited. When it seemed as if he wasn't going to finish the story, JT prompted, "But you met her again?"

"She didn't seem to understand no." Jack spread

his hands on the desk. "She came back and we got to talking. She kept insisting she wanted a job, but I knew what she was really looking for. She wanted her father. But she was willing to settle for a grumpy old man."

"So what are you going to do now?"

"Same as I've been doing. She was crying this morning. She thought I'd be mad. She's pissed at her mom—Hailey has a lot of ground to make up there. But I told her we'd be here for her if she wants us."

"We?"

"You started this, JT. She wants a family and you're part of that."

"No, Dad. I'm not. I'm here for you and then I'm going back to Pittsburgh."

"You told that lie and she grew up believing it. You have a responsibility."

JT came all the way into the room. "I never meant for her to grow up that way. Hailey was supposed to straighten it all out."

"Did you ever check with her? Ask if she did?"

"No."

"So there's a kid who grew up with the idea of you being her dad. So you're not, and I guess now nobody can expect you to be that for her. But I like her and I got used to the idea of being her grandpa. You can be, I don't know, her uncle or something."

"Hailey's not going to want this."

"Hailey lost the right to have a say in what me and Olivia do way back when she left that lie standing. And you lost your right when you ran away and never came back. You both set me and Olivia up, and you can't take it back now."

"Dad. I didn't run away."

"You did. Your mom and I might have been wrong, but you were wrong, too. You shouldn't have left. But you got your feelings hurt and you quit. Same as always."

"I didn't quit anything. I asked you for help and you said no. I asked Hailey to marry me and she said no. What was I supposed to do?"

"Fight. But that's not what you do. You joke around and play around and as soon as things get hard, you quit."

How dare he bring that old accusation up now? *Quitter.* JT left that label behind the night he'd left them behind. He hadn't quit. He'd won.

He looked at his dad one more second, then spun on his heel and left. Jack said something that sounded like "Proving my point," but JT didn't go back. He went straight to his room and threw his duffel on his bed.

These people were all insane. Hailey was living in some fantasy world—a time warp at work and a lie at home, and that was just what he'd found out from seeing her on a handful of occasions. Jack had given up his business and adopted a granddaughter, and was generally acting totally unlike himself. They all wanted JT to do or be or pretend something, and he wasn't up for any of it.

Well, he didn't have to stay here and let these people ruin his life all over again.

He gave the shirt he was folding a savage twist, wishing he could rip the fabric, tear it into pieces. He *didn't* have to stay. That was true. But if he left now, he *was* a quitter. He'd said he would stay and help his dad get back on his feet. He'd promised himself he would take the chance on working things out with the man. If he left now, he'd know that he'd run because being here terrified him.

So he'd stay. For a few more days at least.

CHAPTER SEVEN

HAILEY HAD BACK-TO-BACK appointments the next morning, starting with Tony King and ending with Mrs. Perkins. When she finally handed her morning charts to Debby, she had less than ten minutes to make it to McNulty's house.

She'd dressed carefully that morning in a pair of brown pants and a fitted red cotton shirt with brown piping. Cynthia, who worked exclusively in track-suits, liked to poke fun at her wardrobe, but Hailey felt more confident when she dressed up. As long as she could move in her clothes, and her shoes were comfortable, she didn't see any reason to dress differently.

She parked her Mustang in Mr. McNulty's driveway. How long had it been since she'd pulled in here? She cut across the lawn and went up the front steps to the deep, wraparound porch. A pile of decking sat at the foot of the steps and a toolbox was open near the hedge. Someone was in the middle of putting in a wheelchair ramp. Which, in her professional opinion, was an excellent idea, if several months too late.

She rang the doorbell and waited. When Mr. McNulty appeared, she was surprised to see Olivia behind him.

"Mr. McNulty said you weren't going to come, but I told him you'd be here," her daughter said as she swung the screen door open. "She wasn't even late," she added, sounding perfectly at home in the house and with the man. But also, as if she'd had perfect trust in her mother, which gave Hailey hope that she'd been right to agree to see Mr. McNulty.

"Another three minutes and she would have been," Jack said. "And that's without consulting Mr. Atomic Clock."

They both snickered and Hailey had the idea they were joking about JT, but she didn't get it. What she did get was that her daughter and Mr. McNulty were acting like old friends. So that meant either JT still hadn't talked to his dad or the man didn't care that he wasn't actually Olivia's grandfather. Hailey gripped the leather strap of her purse until the buckle dug into her palm.

She stepped into the living room, feeling oddly dislocated as if she'd stepped back in time. She and JT hadn't been here much during the months they'd dated. His parents had been fighting bitterly that year and he'd tried to spend as little time as possible at his house. But she'd been here enough that it was all familiar—from the dark, brooding walls offset by Craftsman-style woodwork to the many pieces of Melanie's art on display. A large nude portrait of a woman hung over the fireplace and Hailey stared at it for a minute, arrested by the idea of something like that in a Cedar Street living room. When she realized the woman was Melanie, she quickly averted her eyes. She hadn't known JT's mom well, and didn't think she'd need to further her acquaintance in that particularly intimate way ever.

Olivia was still standing near Jack. Hailey felt the distance between her and her daughter widen. Her girl was here, with these people she didn't know, and if she wasn't careful, Olivia would have a whole life built up that didn't include the mother who'd lied to her.

Hailey cleared her throat. "So, I have paperwork and then we need someplace I can do an exam."

Just at that moment JT came down the hall. He was wearing jeans again, this time with a black T-shirt printed with a picture of a Frisbee and the words Huck It Deep. "We have the dining room set up as his bedroom," he said. "I think we can work in there."

"*We* aren't working anywhere," Jack stated. "This is a private consultation." He backed his wheelchair up and started to pass JT.

"But don't you want—"

"No."

JT turned to Hailey for support. "Tell him I'm allowed to be in there. He's my dad."

"If you were the patient and you were a minor, then he'd be obligated to be with you. It doesn't work the other way around."

JT put his hands on his hips. "I don't suppose I get to hear the results of the evaluation then, do I?"

"Not unless your dad okays it. Or he's incompetent."

"Which I don't," Jack said. "And I'm not."

JT opened his mouth, but Jack pointed a finger at him. "Not."

Hailey checked with Olivia. "I guess you'll still be here when I get finished?"

"We're having brunch after," Olivia answered.

Of course, Hailey thought. How silly to even ask.

She followed Mr. McNulty through the living room and closed the dining-room door. She put her purse on the floor and then opened her messenger style laptop bag. "I'm going to need a history and then we can see what's what," she said as she booted the machine.

Mr. McNulty nodded.

She asked him to tell her about his injuries, and took careful notes as he recounted what he remembered about the accident. He'd had a Subaru station wagon up on the lift in the garage. He didn't realize that the lock on the lift mechanism hadn't fully engaged. He was entirely under the car when he heard the first snapping sounds and he'd rolled, desperately scrambling to get out of the way.

His hands clenched into fists on his knees as he spoke. Luckily for him the lift had a backup safety that had engaged, so he wasn't crushed by the dropping car. But he'd been caught by the back wheel and had sustained serious injuries to both knees and his left hip.

He'd had surgery on his knees and some rehab in the hospital, but hadn't gone back since he'd been home. He could get the records sent to her if she wanted them.

Hailey was more familiar with accidental injury than most. But stories like this one still affected her deeply. The worst thing about Mr. McNulty's story, though, was the way he told it. He was very detached, almost as if he was recounting something he'd read in a newspaper. She knew quite a bit about compensation and coping mechanisms, and she wouldn't be surprised to find Mr. McNulty still had feelings about the accident that he hadn't fully processed.

She took other information from him and then explained that she'd like to examine him. She helped him into the bed and brought her laptop closer so she could take notes as she worked.

She focused on his body, trying to see him just as a patient and nothing more. He responded to her requests, but didn't really speak to her. When she was finished she had a clear picture of what his rehab was going to be like.

"Mr. McNulty—"

"Call me Jack."

"Okay. Jack. As I'm sure you're aware, you suffered serious trauma to your legs. The neglect over the past few months has exacerbated the original damage. But with hard work, you can turn things around. You can definitely get yourself mobile again. It's up to you to decide if you're willing to put the work in."

"I'll work," he said.

"You didn't before. What changed?"

"JT came home. Olivia said I should call you."

Hailey closed her laptop, avoiding eye contact with him. "I'd prefer to give you a referral to someone else."

"Because of me, Olivia or JT?"

She closed her eyes briefly. Straightforward people were the ones she found hardest to deal with. "All three. Plus me."

"Olivia is a nice kid. I'm glad she came and found me," he said. "I'd like to work with you."

"Why?" Hailey asked.

"Olivia told me you're the best. Is that a good enough reason?"

Hailey folded her arms. She barely knew Jack but knew he had a goal here. He'd pegged her right, though. If Olivia wanted her to work with him, was Hailey going to say no? *Not without a better reason than "I'm not sure it's a good idea."*

"It's not a good enough reason, but it's pretty good blackmail."

Jack settled in his chair. "So we're square?"

"If you do the work."

His eyes flicked to the side, but he refocused quickly. "I'll do the work."

"I want to see you at Viva. I only do home visits for folks who aren't able to come in."

"Half the time here, half the time there."

"Three weeks and we're going to reevaluate."

Jack stuck his hand out. "Deal."

"Before we shake I have a condition of my own."

He nodded.

"Olivia seems to like you." An understatement, but it was as much as Hailey was willing to admit right then. "Don't mess with her. If you're playing some game with JT or whatever, tell me now and let me take her home before she gets hurt."

"No games. I told you," Jack said. "I like her."

Hailey shook his hand, knowing she'd just agreed to be part of something she didn't fully understand. But the big, puzzling man with the broken body had convinced her she wanted to take this chance.

AS SOON AS THE DOOR HAD CLOSED behind Hailey and Jack, Olivia immediately hunched into a defensive posture. JT wasn't used to being terrifying.

"You know anything about carpentry?" he'd asked her.

She shrugged but her shoulders relaxed enough to encourage him.

"I'm building a ramp. Could use an extra set of hands."

When her eyes lit up and her mouth almost quirked into a smile, he noticed, even though she shut it down fast. All right, then, he wasn't so terrifying after all.

"Let's go."

He'd completed most of the ramp that morning but needed to finish laying the decking. He wanted to test it to be sure the slope and the join with the sidewalk were safe before he put the handrails on. He showed Olivia how to work with the decking and then stood back to let her have a crack at it. Hammering was always fun—no way she'd be able to resist.

She was kneeling in the grass now, not totally at ease with the tool, but doing a half-decent job. The ramp didn't need to look perfect as long as it was safe, so he let her keep going. He went over to the Taurus and opened the door.

"What's your favorite station?" he called to her.

She finished the nail she was working on and sat back on her heels. The knees of her faded jeans were getting wet from the damp grass, but she didn't seem to care.

"WKJY," she said, but then blushed. "It's top-forty. Maybe you want something different."

"I can stand a little Nickelback," JT said. He cranked the volume enough so they could hear it over the hammering. Fall Out Boy wasn't his favorite, but he'd actually paid for an album by The Fresh Prince when he was in high school so he really didn't have any room to talk.

He went back and sat on the porch railing where he could keep an eye on her. "That's a funny shirt," he said. On the front of the sky-blue T-shirt was a graphic showing a row of electric fans, with the message "I Have a Lot of Fans" printed beneath.

"I like yours, too." She set another nail.

"Your mom's not one for the funny T-shirt, is she?"

"My mom doesn't get dressed—she puts on a costume."

"What?"

"It's just how she is. Everything has to be perfect or she gets nervous."

He was surprised to hear Olivia use the word *costume.* That's what he'd always thought about his mom and her clothes. She was constantly trying to manipulate the way people thought about her by dressing for a part. But it sounded as if Olivia thought her mom did the same thing—playing the same role, perfect Hailey, every time.

"When I was in Brownies I made her a shirt for Mother's Day. She wore it to bed but she wouldn't ever have worn it out of the house."

"At least she wore it," he said.

"I guess."

Olivia finished the decking and glanced up. "What next?"

"We have to put on the side rails, but I want to try something first."

She was closing the toolbox when he came back out with the rolling desk chair from Jack's office. "I'll give her a spin first and then you can take a turn."

"You're going to ride that chair down the ramp?" Olivia was staring at him as if he was insane.

"I can't let Jack take the first ride. What if I got the slope wrong?"

She didn't seem convinced.

"Fine, I know the slope is right." JT lifted his

watch. "This has a calculator, too." He pushed the chair closer to the top of the ramp, testing the ease in the swivel. "I really just want to try it. What's the use of building a ramp if you can't mess around with it?" She hadn't moved. "If you have a skateboard we can use that instead," he offered.

Olivia stood off to the side and tucked her hands in the back pockets of her jeans. "Go for it."

JT took a running start and jumped into the chair as he sent it down the ramp. The slope was too gradual for him to build up much speed, but the desk chair spun him around a few times and wound up tossing him out when it hit the edge of the sidewalk.

Olivia ran up. "That was awesome! My turn."

JT pushed the chair back up onto the porch. "You should probably have a helmet," he muttered, but she was already pushing off and whooping as she rattled down the ramp and onto the sidewalk. The chair angled sideways and when it hit the grass it stopped short. Olivia flew out, landing on her knees, and laughing hysterically. "That's hilarious."

Bingo. Exactly the reaction he'd hoped for. It was the first time, JT realized, he'd seen Olivia really laugh. Screw Jack and his quitter crap. JT could be just as nice to this kid as his dad.

HAILEY COULD HEAR Olivia and JT calling to each other even before she opened the door. She and Jack reached the porch just in time to see Olivia launch what looked like a leather desk chair down the ramp, jump out of the chair halfway down, catching the Frisbee JT had thrown, before landing with a thud in the dirt next to the hedges. The chair kept rolling before it upended in the grass near JT.

"Good one!" he called.

Olivia climbed to her feet, dirt clinging to the back of her shirt. "Perfect toss," she said. JT gave her a high five and Olivia's face glowed.

"Olivia, you could have broken your arm. Or cracked your skull," Hailey said.

Olivia scowled at her but JT pointed to the ramp. "The slope is really slight, Hailey. I had to extend the ramp to fit the specs for the Americans with Disabilities office recommendations. There's no way the chair would have gotten enough velocity to do any damage."

Hailey was still caught up in her fear, so the slope or angle or whatever math facts he was spouting didn't really penetrate. What did register was the fact that JT had her daughter doing something ridiculous—he'd never been serious about anything in his life.

"I don't care what specifications you used. You're supposed to be the adult here. You should know better."

"Mom, stop it," Olivia said angrily, but JT nudged her with his elbow.

"I told you we needed helmets."

Olivia giggled, tried to hide it and then elbowed him back while pasting a contrite look on her face. For just for a second, Hailey wondered if this was what it would have been like if she'd said yes when he asked her to marry him. If there'd been three people in their family instead of two. Would he have been a buffer between them, dragging them closer when they butted heads and started to drift apart?

"Bring my chair back up here!" Jack yelled again. "What were you thinking?"

"We were crash testing the ramp. Didn't want you to fall out on your way down," JT said, seemingly unaffected by Jack's reaction. "Why don't you take a test run?"

"Not without the handrails," Hailey said quickly.

"I don't know what you built it for, anyway," Jack groused.

"I built it," JT said, "so you can leave the house under your own power if you want to."

"Who told you to bring my desk chair out here?"

"You weren't exactly using it," JT pointed out.

Jack glared at the ramp, then at JT, then at his chair. "Bring it back inside," he repeated, before he went in and slammed the door.

Olivia picked the chair up, subdued.

"Don't worry about him, kid," JT said. "He's mad at me. I shouldn't have made that crack about the chair."

But JT's jaw was tight and Hailey saw him throw a hard glance toward the front door. She had a feeling Jack was going to hear from his son about his attitude.

"I'll be back on Monday," she said. "We agreed to

three weeks of half time here, half time at Viva. One of you can call and have Debby set up the appointments."

"How does he seem?" JT asked, walking closer. "Is he going to get better?"

"That's really up to him," she said. "It depends if he shows up and does the work."

"He's never backed down from anything in his life."

Hailey blinked. Did JT really think that? "Not before the accident," she said carefully. Sometimes families needed an outside observer to help them see what was really going on. "He's been in that chair for six months. Something's keeping him there."

It was JT's turn to blink. "My dad's afraid?"

"I don't know what it is. But most people, they don't ignore their needs like that. When someone does, there's usually a deeper issue." She pulled her purse higher on her shoulder. "He's on the ball now, though. So that's a good sign."

Olivia's return from taking in the chair cut off their conversation. "Tell Mr. McNulty I'll be back another time, okay? He's not up for brunch right now."

JT nodded. The three of them crossed the yard to the driveway. JT snapped off the radio and closed the door of the Taurus. "See you Monday, then."

Hailey waited until he'd gone back to the house before she asked her daughter if she'd like to grab a bite together.

"No," Olivia said.

Hailey wasn't sure if she wanted to sigh or kick something.

JT PUT THE HANDRAILS ON the ramp and thought about…well…too many things. By the time he was finished, he was sweaty and irritated, and his foot was sore where he'd dropped the end of a railing section on it.

He went inside, but Jack was in his office with the door closed. Around dinnertime JT knocked on the door and asked his dad if he wanted pizza, but didn't get an answer. He said he was sorry about the chair comment but there was no response.

He ended up making a sandwich and eating it on the back porch. He brought his telescope down and spent a few hours messing around, staring into the sky. His dad banged around, but he didn't seem to need help so JT didn't go in. He heard the dining-room door close once again a few minutes later and assumed his dad had gone to bed. Lying on his back, JT let the cool night air brush over him, yet was still unsettled.

A car pulled into the driveway and he got up to see if it was his brother, but it was Hailey.

"Hey," he said.

She fiddled with the car keys in her hand. "Can we talk for a minute?"

He wasn't sure if his dad was asleep and he didn't want Jack eavesdropping, because he had no idea why Hailey was here. So he led her around the

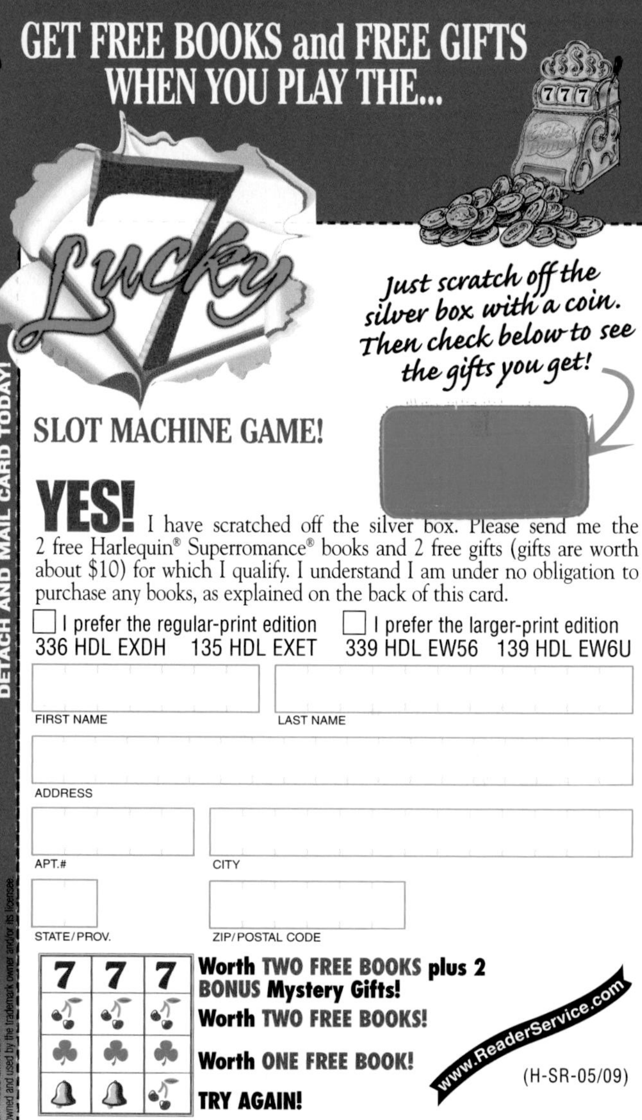
GET FREE BOOKS and FREE GIFTS
WHEN YOU PLAY THE...
Lucky 7
SLOT MACHINE GAME!
Just scratch off the silver box with a coin. Then check below to see the gifts you get!
YES! I have scratched off the silver box. Please send me the 2 free Harlequin® Superromance® books and 2 free gifts (gifts are worth about $10) for which I qualify. I understand I am under no obligation to purchase any books, as explained on the back of this card.
I prefer the regular-print edition
336 HDL EXDH 135 HDL EXET
I prefer the larger-print edition
339 HDL EW56 139 HDL EW6U
FIRST NAME
LAST NAME
ADDRESS
APT.#
CITY
STATE/PROV.
ZIP/POSTAL CODE
Worth TWO FREE BOOKS plus 2 BONUS Mystery Gifts!
Worth TWO FREE BOOKS!
Worth ONE FREE BOOK!
TRY AGAIN!
www.ReaderService.com
(H-SR-05/09)
DETACH AND MAIL CARD TODAY!

house, limping a little, and sat on the steps of the porch. She sat next to him, the pale fabric of her pants a brighter patch in the dim light.

"Did you do something to your foot?" Hailey asked.

"Dropped a board on it."

"I can check it if you'd like."

"It's fine."

"Is that your old telescope?" She was nervous about being here, and dreaded starting the conversation.

"Yep." He leaned back on his elbows. "You came over so I could show you the Big Digger?"

"I…ah…I wanted to talk about Olivia. Your dad acts as if he wants to continue a relationship with her."

"He does. Despite his tantrum this morning, he likes her. I guess she'll have to suffer with his bad moods, same as the rest of us.

"She… I think she misses having grandparents. And we don't have anybody else." *God this is hard.*

"Okay," he said slowly.

Hailey smoothed a wrinkle in her pants down from the top of her thigh. "I want to know if that's okay with you. If she and your dad spend time together."

JT dipped his head backward, his eyes on the sky. "God, Hailey, it's a little late to be asking me this, isn't it?" He got to his feet and shoved his hands into the pockets of his jeans. "Maybe you should have sorted this out back when you sent your kid birthday cards from me."

She startled. "How—"

"She told my dad."

"I'm sorry, JT. I know I made a mess of everything, but Olivia and your dad…they worked things out. Are you going to be okay with that?"

He spun around. "I don't have a whole lot of choice, do I?"

"I'm sorry," she repeated.

"The part I don't get is why?" JT's eyes were shadowed in the dusk, but his voice sank and his posture was stiff. "I asked you to marry me and you said no. If you wanted Olivia to have a dad so much, why didn't you accept?"

She stood up, too. "I'd already made one mistake and I couldn't make another one."

"Right. I was too young."

"JT, you were flunking French," she said. "You planned to go to the University of Vermont specifically because it was a party school. And you told me more than once that the best lesson you ever learned from your parents was to avoid marriage. You weren't exactly the ideal candidate for a husband and father."

"You know what? I get that, sort of. But the part that sucks is that when my parents kicked me out I had to grow up. And all that stuff that scared you about me? I ditched it. I did it for me." He took a step toward her. "But I could have done it for you." The way he stood, his hands in his pockets, shoulders drawn up, made her wish she could have let him. But she hadn't loved him.

"That just proves my point. I didn't know you or what you were capable of, and you didn't know me. We'd have been married before we even really knew ourselves, let alone each other."

Neither of them spoke for a minute.

"So you underestimated me. What didn't I know about you?"

"That I was sleeping with someone else, for starters."

JT jerked back, his chin tucked down. "Well, I guess I figured that out." He tightened his jaw and straightened his shoulders. "You didn't come here to talk about that, anyway," he said. "I like Olivia. If she wants to be my dad's foster granddaughter or whatever, I'm not going to get in the way."

"Even if it means you have to see me?"

"I'm over that, Hailey. Don't worry about it."

But if he was really over it, he wouldn't keep bringing it up, would he? She wished she could make him understand that what he thought they'd had hadn't been real. She'd been pretending with him, pretending to the world while she was sneaking off with Trevor. But she'd never been able to face that part of herself, never mind show it to someone else. She hadn't even told Sarah exactly what it had been like to be with Trevor. Every time she got too close to the memories, she shied away.

She would have liked to apologize again, but she didn't think it would help anything. So she whispered, "Thanks. For Olivia," before walking back to her car. He didn't follow her.

CHAPTER EIGHT

JT GOT UP EARLY ON Saturday. He'd been getting a lot of extra sleep since he'd been here, and didn't have the normal deadline pressures he was used to at RoboGen. His dreams were still crazy, though. Last night he, Olivia, Hailey and Jack had been in Jack's wheelchair, trying to maneuver across a tightrope. JT was trying to tell them they should be wearing helmets, but he couldn't force the words out, and Jack pushed them all off the platform. The falling sensation had woken JT and he couldn't get back to sleep. He lay on his back, staring up at the bottom of the top bunk.

The more he thought about the conversation he'd had with Hailey, the more irritated he got. She was so hung up on what they used to be, who they'd been or not been when they were together. He didn't see why she couldn't let all that go. Granted, he'd been an idiot in high school, but he'd changed. She didn't seem willing to either explain what had happened back then or let it go. And she really didn't seem able to let him get to know her now.

When he went downstairs, Jack was up, too, so

JT helped him dress; the routine was becoming more familiar and he didn't feel so strange about being up close with his dad. He'd put grab bars in the bathroom and Jack was able to do more on his own now.

"You want breakfast?" JT asked. "I can make scrambled eggs."

"I'll be out in a minute."

They sat at the table, a plate of eggs each, a pile of toast in the middle and the pot of coffee close at hand. JT watched the numbers flip on his watch. For seven excruciating, perfectly calibrated atomic minutes, they didn't exchange a single word.

"Olivia seems to like you," Jack said.

"She's a nice kid." JT swallowed a mouthful of coffee. "You shouldn't yell like that when she's around. You scared her."

"Thanks for that tip."

"What are you so angry about?" JT asked.

Jack snorted. "I'm in a wheelchair. My business is closed. I'm finding out I made a lot of bad choices in my life and I can't do a thing to change them. There's a whole bunch of things on the list. And to top it all off, while I'm inside being poked and prodded and praised for lifting my goddamn leg half an inch off the bed, you're outside using my furniture for carnival rides. All right?" He pushed back from the table. "Where's the broom?"

JT wasn't sure, because he was far from an expert in Jack McNulty body language, but if he had to guess, he'd say his dad's feelings were hurt.

Was he jealous that JT and Olivia had been messing around together? Was that even possible?

"In the hall closet, I guess. What do you want it for?"

Jack didn't answer, just continued out of the kitchen. JT raised his voice. "Dad?"

"Housecleaning!"

JT had just finished loading the dishwasher when there was a crash from the living room and then silence. He bolted out of the kitchen and was halfway down the hall when Jack started swearing. At least he wasn't dead, JT thought as he skidded into the living room.

The wheelchair was overturned on the brick hearth and his dad was on the floor, a large flat board on top of him. He was thrashing and cursing, and JT hollered, "Stop, Dad! Give me a second." As he raced over, he glanced at the ceiling, because the only logical answer he could think of was that the ceiling had given way. But everything was fine up there. The mess seemed confined to the floor.

"Get this goddamn thing off me!" Jack bellowed.

As soon as he lifted the edge of the panel, JT realized what it was. Shifting his grip to the very edge of the frame, he swallowed, then levered up and moved his mother's nude portrait off his father.

It was too big for him to get his arms around so he moved to one side and, being very careful not to touch any of his mom's *bits,* he slid the painting across the floor until he could lean it, Melanie side in, against the wall.

Jack was still sprawled on the floor, one arm over his eyes. JT wished he could have shut his own. He'd been living with the painting but had been very careful not to really see it. He was worried his close encounter had left him scarred for life.

"Hang on a sec while I get your chair," he said. He grabbed the wheelchair, but when he tried to push it, he realized the broom was jammed in the spokes of the wheel. He untangled the broom handle and pushed the chair to his dad.

When he had it next to Jack and had set the brakes, he leaned down and grabbed him around the waist to help him up. While he was used to physical proximity with his dad, this felt different. Jack was stiff, and if he'd been anyone else, JT would have thought he was embarrassed. But JT couldn't remember ever seeing his dad embarrassed. Not even when he should have been.

"Are you hurt?" he asked.

"No," his dad answered curtly.

"Were you cleaning the painting?"

Jack didn't answer. But he didn't push his chair away either. Which was weird. The man was the king of ending conversations by leaving. What the hell was going on?

JT gestured at the portrait. Even though he hated the thing and felt nauseous at the idea of touching it again, he asked, "You want me to put it back up?"

"I took the damn thing down. Why the hell would I want you to put it back?"

Huh.

"You..." He wasn't sure what to say. If he was reading the situation correctly, his dad had just used a broom to knock a life-size nude portrait of his mother off the wall and onto himself.

What the hell was the correct response to a situation like that?

"You want to hang it somewhere else? In your room?"

Jack shot him a look of disgust. The one that was usually coupled with the word *moron.* But when he spoke, his voice was rough, and again, if it had been anyone but Jack, JT would have thought he was upset. "What I want is for you to burn it. Can you do that for me, son?"

"Dad, what are you talking about?"

"I'm talking about getting rid of that thing once and for all."

"But why? Why now?"

Jack glanced at the painting and then up at the blank spot over the fireplace. "Because it's time. You mom made a lot of decisions and I went along with them. She was...well...I was so tangled up with her I never... You know how it was. But I'm doing things differently now."

Then he did leave. He took the broom and went into his office, slamming the door so hard his mom's portrait slid down to the floor with a loud crack.

Perfect. Now he had to dispose of an oversize painting of his naked mother. JT pulled out his phone and punched in his brother's number.

"Charlie?" he said. "Dad needs a favor. He said you should come over."

HAILEY WAS LOCKING the doors at Viva late Saturday afternoon when her cell phone rang. She pulled it out and glanced at the caller ID.

"JT?" she said.

"I found Olivia's backpack. She must have left it here the other morning."

"Thanks," Hailey answered. "I'll let her know."

He took too long to reply, and the silence dragged out a long awkward beat. She knew there was something else.

"I wasn't snooping," he said. "Believe me, I have no interest in a teenage girl's backpack. But it wasn't zipped and I kicked it accidentally when I was moving…something…and it spilled and some stuff came out. I think you should see it."

Oh, God. This was exactly what every parent was afraid of. "JT, what is it? Drugs?"

"What?" He sounded startled. "What? No. Your yearbook."

"My yearbook?"

There was another one of those long pauses. "I'm not saying I know one thing about what you should do. But I think it would be good if you saw what she was doing with it."

"I'm at Viva. I can swing by on my way home."

"I'm actually on my way there," JT said. "Charlie's here working on a project, so I'm taking a break."

She punched a few songs up in the jukebox while she waited—Ricky Nelson, Peggy Lee, Bing Crosby, The Platters and the Everly Brothers. While "Bye Bye Love" played, she sorted the hand weights and reorganized them from heaviest to lightest. JT knocked on the front door in the lull between one song ending and the next record dropping. She hurried to let him in.

He had the backpack in his right hand. "I zipped it up. Sorry," he said, as she fumbled to get the bag open.

The yearbook was in there, tucked between a black sketchpad and a Phillies baseball cap. She pulled it out. He was right. It was hers, from her senior year.

He tapped the cover. "Turn to the senior portraits part."

She leafed ahead and saw that the pages of the senior section were full of notes. She sank onto the bench in the reception area and stared in dismay.

The handwriting was Olivia's, the distinctive slant to her cursive familiar from countless school essays. Olivia had been doing research on the boys, making notes next to their pictures. Notes related to their likelihood of being her father.

Andy Dickson was on the first page. Hailey barely remembered him, a quiet, dark-haired kid.... He'd taken a friend of hers to the senior prom and had rented a stretch limousine. Next to his picture Olivia had added a question mark with the note, "Married. Florida."

Franklin Gallagher had two question marks with the note, "Cute. Preppy-type. Yes? Ask Mrs. Finley."

Marshall Harrison had a note that cross-referenced page 37. When Hailey flipped there, she saw herself and Marshall laughing at the Homecoming pep rally. She went back to the portraits. Picture after picture had a short collection of details scribbled in the margins.

"She'd make a good detective, wouldn't she?" JT said. "I mean, I don't know if Marshall is actually cute anymore, but she got a lot of information."

"I don't understand how she could have found all this...."

"Facebook? Google? There's stuff out there about almost anyone."

Hailey turned to the page with JT's picture. Olivia had crossed him out with a dark X, but then had erased it. The lines still showed and his mouth was smudged from too much eraser pressure, making his smile more crooked than usual. Next to his picture was the note, "No." Underneath it, though, Hailey saw where another note had been erased. That one read, "Olivia Maddox McNulty."

"I guess she didn't know what to do with me," JT said quietly. He sat next to Hailey.

She closed the book. Feeling a tear slide down her face, she quickly wiped it away.

"What are you doing, Hailey? Why can't you tell her?"

She shook her head. She used to know. It used to be perfectly clear. But then it all got messed up and she honestly didn't know anymore.

"I wanted her to be happy."

"So why not tell her the truth?"

"Because it won't make her happy."

JT took that in. "The truth must really be something, then."

"Trust me," she said.

"I do." He closed his eyes. "I know I shouldn't. But about this. I do. I always have."

Hailey turned to face him. The JT she remembered was still there, in the laugh lines around his eyes and the generous mouth, and the rebellious waves of hair spiking out behind his ears. But he was more now.... If only she could lean on him, open up to him, let him share her worries and her hopes. Get to know the man he was.

But she couldn't.

If she opened up to him, told him about Trevor and how messed up their relationship had been, he'd never understand. She knew he hated Trevor for the affair he'd had with Melanie. That affair had almost destroyed Melanie and Jack's marriage. How could she tell JT that she'd been little better than Trevor because she'd known he was married but hadn't stopped herself from sleeping with him?

She'd been trying so hard to get Olivia to trust her, to believe that it was right to keep Trevor out of their lives, and she'd gotten nothing but grief. And here was JT. Even after everything she'd done to him, he was still able to trust her. There was something inside him that was generous enough to believe in her.

There wasn't any way she could explain to him how much that meant to her.

She leaned forward and, putting a palm on either side of his face, kissed him. It was brief, a brush of her lips on his. She saw the surprise and then the swift heat in his eyes even as she sat back. "Thank you," she whispered in a shaking voice.

"Hailey," he breathed, his voice caught in his throat. He looked at her, so perfect, so much the same girl he'd loved. But he knew now there were hidden parts of her.

She leaned in again and her lips were firmer this time, leaving wet heat on his mouth. He groaned, catapulted right back into that hormonal overdrive he thought he'd left behind around the time he'd bought his first legal drink.

Her hair was down, lying in soft waves on her shoulders, making her look even more beautiful, emphasizing the high, gorgeous curve of her forehead. She was older, her intelligence carried with more confidence, but she was still Hailey Maddox.

He didn't trust her. But he'd never been able to turn her down.

So he leaned closer, and when she didn't pull away, he went for it.

Her mouth was soft under his at first, and the kiss started like the gentle one she'd given him. But then her lips opened and she pushed forward to close the space between them, and her breasts were pressing into his chest. Just like that, without any transition, they weren't kissing, they were making out.

He slid the yearbook down the bench and hitched closer so he could put both arms around her, one hand on the back of her head, stroking the smooth fall of hair down to the loose, curling tips, and the other lower on her ribs, where he thought he could feel her heart hammering. Or was it his? Who could tell when there wasn't a half inch of space between them?

He was kissing Hailey and it was just as hot and desperate as it had been when they were both seventeen and panting their way toward something neither of them really understood.

She put her arms around him, holding him, winding her hands in the back of his hair. *God.*

He nipped at the corner of her lip before kissing his way across her jaw and down to the sensitive skin of her neck. When she lifted her chin, baring her throat, he shivered, because she wanted this. Wanted him. He pressed her closer and moved back to her mouth, savoring the sweet intensity of the kiss.

Hailey closed her eyes. She hadn't expected this, but surrendered completely to it. The pressure on her back, the intense prickles of sensation on her head where he was stroking her hair, his lips on her mouth, her jaw, her neck, her skin…it was all so much feeling. She hadn't felt like this, felt anything this much, in so long. She did not want to stop kissing JT McNulty.

To stifle her thoughts, because she didn't want thoughts, she wanted to be with him in this moment, she slid against him, moving on the bench until she could slip one leg over his and press herself against him. The rough fabric of his jeans on her bare leg under her skirt was hopelessly stimulating. She ran her hands down his back, reveling in the interplay of muscle and bone, until she could hook her fingers in the sides of his jeans and pull.

"Where do you want me to be?" he murmured against her mouth.

"Closer. Here," she whispered back.

He shifted and then, with his hands on her bottom, scooped her up to sit on his lap. He was hard and she pressed against his erection, loving the feeling of him, loving that she'd done that to him. She tipped her head back and he kissed his way down her neck, the intensity of the sensation driving her crazy. His hands slid up her legs and held her close, skin on skin covered by the silky slide of her skirt.

"So perfect," he breathed. "You're absolutely perfect."

He'd always said that, called her perfect. But it hadn't been true then and certainly wasn't true now. She kissed him harder to make him stop talking.

He moved his hands higher, squeezing and caressing her thighs, and she went back to enjoying kissing him. This. Just exactly this. She loved it.

Loved everything about this moment, wrapped up and around JT in the quiet and dark of the locked-up center.

She didn't know how long they stayed like that, but when she pulled back her lips were chapped and her mouth felt swollen. She couldn't do this with him. He was her past and she'd always appreciate what he'd done for her, but they couldn't have a future. She wasn't going to tell Olivia about Trevor and she and JT couldn't unravel what had happened between them without that piece. And he still didn't see her—just who he thought she was.

She pushed against him and then stood up, smoothing her skirt down and pressing the neckline of her shirt back into place.

She stood still, feeling each of her nerves settle from high alert back to a more normal state as her skin cooled and she readjusted to being just her not part of her and him.

She put her hand up to her lips and softly traced them.

JT stood and tried to put his arms back around her, but she stopped him. "I should go. Olivia will be wondering where I am."

"Used to have to go because of curfew." He dropped his arms and she could see that he was confused, maybe hurt. She didn't want to hurt him again.

"Things changed," she said.

"Sure did," he answered softly.

She let him out and then locked the door behind

him. As his headlights swept the front of the building, she raised a hand. "Bye," she whispered.

When she got home, Sarah was sitting on a lounge chair on the patio. She was wearing yoga pants and a sweatshirt and was just sitting, not reading or even listening to her iPod. "Sarah?" Hailey said. "Is something wrong?"

"No."

If that was the truth, Hailey was Wilma Flintstone.

"You want to come in?"

"No."

"Did something happen? I thought Erik was getting home tonight."

"He did. He's inside." Sarah seemed to give herself a shake. "Are you going to the St. Pete's fund-raiser on Friday? I know we talked about it, but I can't remember what you said."

"I said I would go."

"Good. Erik has to leave town again and I need a date."

"Thanks. I think." Hailey sat on the end of the chair. She couldn't see Sarah, but the fact that her friend was out here in the dark without turning the lights on was odd. And that she'd skate this close to admitting everything wasn't hunky-dory in her life was even more odd. Sarah pretty much defined the idea of relentlessly cheerful. "Are you okay?"

"I'm fine." She crossed her legs and sat up. Sarah looked like a kid, in her loose pants, her knees bent and her short, wavy hair caught back in a wide headband. "Erik is always busy. I get frustrated, I guess. But I made my bed, so I'll just have to learn to enjoy lying in it alone."

"Sarah?"

"Sorry. I'll be fine tomorrow." She dug up a smile and straightened her shoulders. "Where were you? Please tell me you were out doing something fantastic."

"I had appointments all afternoon."

"Work? That's what you're giving me?" Sarah looked put out. "Couldn't you have at least made up something fantastic?"

Hailey felt a sudden rush of giddiness because somehow, she wasn't sure how, she had managed a fantastic something. "JT came by. He kissed me."

Sarah leaned forward, her eyes shining. "If you're making this up I need you to swear never to tell me. Give me every fantastic detail."

"Olivia left her backpack at his house and he returned it."

"That's not a very good lie." Sarah looked confused for a minute. "You *are* making this up, right?" She studied Hailey and then a grin crept slowly across her face. "You're not making it up. Tell me."

"He kissed me."

"And?" Sarah prompted.

"And what?"

"A) he kissed me and it was worse than kissing wallpaper or B) he kissed me and time stopped and I might never recover or—"

"B."

"Oh. My. God." Sarah grabbed her hands. "Time stopped?"

"Metaphorically."

"I'm so glad you live here," her friend said with something close to her normal good cheer. "This is what I needed—someone I can live vicariously through."

Hailey was unclear why anyone would want to live through her, least of all Sarah. Hailey's life wasn't anything anyone else would want. Hadn't been for years. But then she remembered how JT's hands felt on her back and how she'd wanted to let him do more but had stopped him. And what if she hadn't? She shivered. What if they didn't have that history between them and she was just getting to know him?

"I'm not certain there's going to be any *living* vicariously, exactly. The kissing was nice—" Hailey had to work to say nice and not bone-shaking amazing "—but it was just one time, not an ongoing lifestyle change."

"You can kiss him again."

"I couldn't. Or shouldn't, at least."

Sarah shook her head emphatically. "No. You have to. I need to live vicariously through someone and you're here, which means I can get the details fast. And you admitted the kissing was great so it will be worthwhile vicarious living. You're the one. I don't know anyone else who can do this."

"Do what? Kiss JT?"

"No. Start fresh." Sarah's voice had changed

and Hailey had the feeling she wasn't joking anymore. "I know you guys are all messed up because of Trevor and the pretending about JT. But you have a chance. To go over your list of what-ifs and see if any are yes ma'ams."

"I don't know, Sarah." If they started fresh, she'd have to let JT get to know her. She knew what he saw when he looked at her, she worked hard enough to project that image. Once he found out that underneath she'd made enormous mistakes, had such big doubts, didn't even know how to talk to her own daughter anymore, well, he'd be out the door.

"You can't sit there and tell me you don't wonder. I know you wonder about JT. Find out."

"And what then? After the…"

"After the additional kissing," Sarah said with a triumphant smirk.

"After the kissing. What next?"

Sarah let out a soft breath and then stood, dusting the seat of her pants as she looked up at her dark bedroom window. "What next? You're the lucky one who's still finding that out, Hailey. The rest of us already know." She started to walk away but paused. "Find out. So you don't always wonder."

If only it were that easy. It was the truth that gave her problems, not the wondering.

The two women hugged for a long beat, the quiet rippling of the pool the only sound. Hailey squeezed Sarah and then let her go. "You know what's weird?"

Sarah shrugged. "People who believe in alien abduction?"

"That, too. But it's weird that I don't remember meeting you—you've just always been my best friend." Hailey stroked Sarah's hair. "Thanks for being you."

Sarah blinked fast and pushed her headband back, settling it behind her ears. "You're probably the only person in the world who would ever say that," she said. "I'm going in before we break out the tequila and get all sloppy and decide we need tattoos that say 'Sisters Forever' or something."

They hugged again quickly and then Sarah crossed the yard to the house. Hailey watched her friend weave through the furniture on the patio before opening the white wooden door. She waved as she turned out the kitchen lights.

A car door slammed in front of the house and Olivia came into view, walking slowly backward, waving to someone on the street. Hailey wondered where her daughter would be in fifteen years. Would she know who she was, and be comfortable in her skin like JT, or would she still be trying to figure herself out and holding on to an image she wasn't sure she'd ever wanted in the first place, like Hailey?

"Mom?" Olivia called. "Why are you out here?"

"I was talking to Sarah."

"Oh."

Olivia was wearing that T-shirt with the fans again.

"Did I ever tell you I like that shirt?"

"No. As a matter of fact, you told me you weren't

sure people would understand that this was an ironic shirt and you suggested I should return it."

Of course that's what she'd said. It was exactly how her brain worked. "Sorry," Hailey said. "That was bad advice."

"I didn't listen to you, so no big deal."

Olivia sounded suspicious but not angry. And for them these days, this would count as an Olympic-length conversation. But Hailey couldn't ignore the yearbook issue. She touched Olivia's wrist. "We need to talk about something. Let's go inside."

They settled in the living room, Olivia sitting stiffly on the couch. Hailey handed her the backpack. "You forgot this at Mr. McNulty's. JT brought it by." Her hand drifted to her lips.

"Tell him thanks," Olivia said, but her neck was flushed, a telltale sign that she was embarrassed.

"It... The bag opened and I saw this." Hailey held up the yearbook.

Olivia looked up quickly. "He didn't see it, did he?"

"We didn't know not to open it. I'm sorry."

"Mom!" she said. "Why would you snoop in my stuff? Why would you let him?"

Hailey leaned forward. "It wasn't snooping. It's my yearbook. I just opened it randomly."

"It was in my bag. You had no right."

Olivia grabbed the book. Her daughter felt embarrassed and violated enough just then. Hailey didn't need to make a big deal about the disrespect, or quibble over rights. Olivia needed to keep a little dignity so maybe she would be able to talk to her mother.

"Olivia," she said as she sat next to her, but then she stopped.

Olivia held the book tight against her chest. In her jeans, T-shirt and old red Converse sneakers she looked about six years old, and all Hailey saw was her daughter's vulnerability.

Olivia's voice was surprisingly composed when she said, "You didn't love him, did you?"

"Didn't...what?" Had she been so obvious? Could Olivia tell she'd been kissing JT?

"My dad. You didn't love him, did you?" Her eyes, partially covered by her hair, were fixed on Hailey. If Hailey admitted she hadn't loved Trevor, if Olivia knew their relationship had been more about power on his side and risk on hers, what would that do to her daughter's view of her? To her daughter's self-esteem?

"That's complicated, Olivia." She rested her hand on the cushion between them, wishing she could reach for her little girl as she would have a few years ago. "But no matter how I felt about him, I got you out of our relationship and you're the best part of my life."

Olivia opened the book and flipped through the pages slowly. "He's not in here, is he? I won't find him here no matter how hard I look."

"I wish you could trust me," Hailey said.

"But you don't trust *me*. There's something wrong with him, isn't there? If he was one of these boys, you'd have told me. What was wrong with him?"

Before Hailey could think of an answer, Olivia said, "Was he married?"

Hailey closed her eyes. When Trevor had first started flirting with her she'd been flattered and thrilled. He was a teacher, but young enough that a lot of girls had had crushes on him.

Hailey had been the good girl. An only child of indulgent parents, she'd found her life safe and predictable. Trevor had offered risks and danger, a way to experiment with being someone else. Their relationship was secret and totally separate from reality.

She didn't have to be perfect Hailey with him—he liked it when she was edgy, bad. He'd taken her to clubs where he'd bought her drinks, given her gifts of lingerie and several times had taken her to a hotel in the city overnight. While she did the things she was supposed to with JT—movies, football games, the prom—Trevor had showed her a whole different perspective. It had been a thrill just to know she was doing something her parents would hate.

After she stopped seeing him, she realized what she'd mistaken for love had been the adrenaline-filled excitement of sneaking around. What she'd thought was adult had been stupid and wrong. The things Trevor had asked her to do had been bad judgment or worse on his part.

She'd been so full of the thrill of her secret relationship with Trevor, of feeling grown-up and defiant, that she hadn't even thought about his wife until after they'd slept together the first time.

"He had a wife," she answered Olivia. She felt deeply mortified, but she couldn't pretend to be something better than she really was.

"Did his wife know about you?"

"No," Hailey said. And Trevor had done everything he could do to keep it that way.

"But you knew he was married when you had sex with him." Her daughter pushed on, relentless.

"I made a lot of mistakes, Olivia," she said. "I did things I shouldn't have. I can't expect you to understand, and some of it I'm not willing to discuss. But I do know I was wrong. I would never do something like that again."

"You can have this back." Olivia put the book on the couch next to her. "At least now I know why you won't tell me who he is. If people find out you slept with a married guy they won't think you're so wonderful anymore, will they?" She paused. "You are so selfish."

"Olivia, wait, please," Hailey said, but her daughter had run out of the room, pounding down the hall in her sneakers. The bedroom door slammed.

Hailey picked up the yearbook and leafed through the pages. She was in a lot of the pictures, on the cheerleading squad, student council and in candid shots with JT and Sarah and her other friends. Hailey could see the way she'd worked to seem confident and in control at all times. What she couldn't see was the fear she'd felt that she wasn't good enough, was less than what people saw when they looked at her.

She shut the book abruptly. Walking through the kitchen to the back door, she took the lid off a garbage can. She lifted out the top bag and then dropped the yearbook in, replacing the garbage on top. At least Olivia wouldn't have to see it again. And neither would she.

HE HADN'T BEEN PAYING attention when he pulled his car into the driveway. Instead, he'd been thinking about how it had felt to kiss Hailey. How absolutely amazing she'd felt in his arms. The last person who made him feel this way was his high-school girlfriend, Hailey Maddox.

So, no, he wasn't exactly at Navy SEAL level of attention when he got out of his car, but still, Charlie didn't have to leap out at him, right?

"Get off me," JT said as his brother grabbed his sleeve and then clamped a hand over his mouth before pulling him away from the house, on the other side of his car. When Charlie took his hand away, JT punched him. "What the hell is wrong with you?"

Charlie shoved a stack of papers at him. "Dad said as long as I was burning that…that *thing*…you know, Mom's picture—I should burn these papers too."

"But you didn't burn them because they are a map to a secret treasure and you want my help to dig it up?"

Kissing Hailey had done wonders for his mood.

Charlie didn't appreciate the joke.

"I didn't burn the picture because I couldn't. I mean, honestly, it's nasty but it's our mother. I wrapped it up so I can take it to my place to store it. Then I washed my hands, a lot. I didn't burn the papers because, well, read them."

"It's too—" Charlie snapped a flashlight on and shone the beam on the pages "—dark. Okay, Charlie, you're freaking me out."

His brother waved the light impatiently across the pages. JT started to read.

Holy crap.

He scanned the front page and then quickly flipped to the last page in the stack.

"Holy crap, he signed this. It's dated the day she died," JT breathed. He gaped at Charlie. "They were getting divorced."

His brother nodded. "Why would they do that?"

Charlie sounded bewildered, which was funny. He and JT had lived through the grand disaster that was Melanie and Jack. If anyone would know why they were divorcing, it should be their sons. But that was the irony of their family. Their parents had been so wrapped up in each other, so totally one-without-the-other about their relationship that it was impossible for anyone, even him and Charlie, to imagine them apart.

"It says irreconcilable differences. There aren't any details."

"Did you know?" JT asked.

"No. Neither of them said a word."

"Shutting the garage? Filing for divorce?

Hanging out with Olivia?" JT said. "If he was a teenager I'd search his room for drugs."

"How about asking you to be his nurse?" Charlie took the papers back and folded them down the middle.

Yeah, there was that, too.

"Where is he now?" JT asked.

"He went to bed. I knocked but he didn't answer."

"He does that."

"You going to ask him about this?"

JT nodded. "We have a bunch of things we need to talk about."

"Better you than me." Charlie turned off the flashlight. "Help me put Mom in my car, would you?"

The portrait, wrapped in what he thought was a bedsheet and at least two rolls of duct tape, was leaning against the passenger side of his brother's Mercedes.

"I'd have been happy to help, except you called it 'Mom,'" JT said. But he moved around to take one end. Charlie opened the back door and lifted the other end.

"Slide her in easy."

"Stop that."

With Charlie guiding, JT was able to push the painting in and angle it so that the door would close, thank God. He wouldn't have wanted to help carry it anywhere.

"I'm glad he took that down," JT said. "It creeped me out."

"You and my prom date both. No pictures in front of the mantel for us," Charlie said. "I never understood why he let her hang it up in the first place. It was like she was throwing the affair in his face. Speaking of which, I saw that ass Trevor Meyers last week. He asked me about you."

"He still lives here?"

"He's the principal at the high school now."

"I freaking hate that guy." JT's fist clenched just thinking about him. He and Charlie should have beaten him up the night of the art opening. Or Jack should have. Someone should have taught him a lesson. "I can't believe he talked to you. You guys don't socialize, do you?"

Charlie made a face. "Are you kidding? No," he said. "It was weird. He came up to me at the gym and asked me flat out how long you were staying. Then he said something about Hailey—wanted to know if you were still close with her."

"What'd you tell him?"

"To get the hell away from me."

JT grinned. "Nice."

Charlie left and JT went around to the back porch. He adjusted the telescope until it was aimed in the direction of Mars. This wasn't a good time in the cycle to see the planet with a telescope, so he could barely make it out. But he spent some time looking, anyway.

He hadn't liked the way he'd left things with Hailey. Everything had been pretty damn mutual. But she'd definitely shut him down. Snapped her

Hailey Maddox shields back in place. The question was, did she do it because she was scared or nervous or did she not want him?

Seemed like that was always the question when it came to him and Hailey.

CHAPTER NINE

THEY WERE LATE. NOT just late. In three minutes, Jack McNulty was going to be a no-show. Hailey rechecked at her packed schedule for the day.

"Even if they get here now, my whole day is going to be off," she grumbled. She was irritated about the wasted time, sure. But she was worried about Jack, too. And she couldn't help wondering about the timing. Was JT avoiding her? How big a mistake had it been to kiss him?

"I can try calling," Debby said.

"If he shows up now, it won't help anything." *Would it?*

Debby wrinkled her nose as if she smelled something bad. "I don't know how you can stand to work with him. And JT—how can you even talk to him?"

"What? Why?"

"Olivia," Debby said.

"Oh," Hailey said. "Right."

The other woman clicked the appointment window closed. "I'll call and leave a message about the no-show fee."

Hailey nodded. But inside she felt sick. This was

the first time in years anyone had said anything to her about JT. When he'd first left town a lot of her friends had been furious that he'd left her high and dry with a baby. But the talk tapered off as they went to college and found their own lives. But people still thought he was a jerk. Debby had been the one to say it, but she wouldn't be the only one thinking it.

God. Hailey hoped no one had said anything to him since he'd been back in town. How horrible that her lie was still affecting him this way.

JT LEANED HIS HEAD against the wall outside the locked door of his dad's office. "This is so rude, Dad. She put you on the schedule as a favor."

"I'm not going, so you can stop talking."

JT banged on the door in frustration. "How the hell are you going to get better if you sit in that wheelchair all day?"

"I'm putting my earphones on."

"Dad!"

"Tell me if Olivia comes by."

No matter what JT said after that he got no response. He called Viva and asked for Hailey, but the receptionist said she was with a patient. When he said he was calling to apologize for missing his dad's appointment she said something about a twenty-five dollar cancellation fee. He told her to send the bill to his father. Was Hailey ducking him or was she that busy?

JT should never have agreed to stay here. He

knew how his dad was, and he'd got suckered in because the man had made it seem like he wanted him. But all he'd really wanted was an unpaid servant and someone to yell at through locked doors.

JT went upstairs and turned on his laptop. Terrance had e-mailed him the specs for the NASA bid. He deleted them but then dragged the message out of the trash and back into his inbox. He opened the file and started reading.

Before too long he'd pulled up a new file and started making notes. By the time he'd got through the bid materials, he had seven pages of notes and a graphics file with a rudimentary sketch in it.

He closed the files and left the graphic up. Then he clicked the button that started his sketch rotating in the 3-D space on his screen. What would that feel like? he wondered. To work on this bid and, if they won it, to have his design—something he'd dreamed up—out there in space?

Freaking amazing, that's what he figured it would feel like.

He pulled out his cell phone and called Terrance.

"Who else is going after this NASA project?" he asked.

"It's a closed bid. They don't tell you."

"But you know."

"Glenn Jordan. Given. I heard Alan Martin. That group from Texas—they won the Cal Tech bid last year…."

"Synch," JT said.

"Right. Them. That's all Jeannie dug up. There might be another one or two under the radar."

"You really think we have a chance?"

"Why would I be pushing so hard if I didn't think we had a chance?"

JT paced to the window and stared out, not really seeing anything outside. "Because Glenn's doing it?"

Terrance had never forgiven the other man for leaving them abruptly and starting his own firm.

"I wouldn't risk what we've built just to get back at him."

JT wished he could be sure of that.

"A lot of those guys, though," JT said, "they've been around forever. And we're… I mean… I didn't…"

"Please tell me this isn't about your degree."

"The bid committee will care about it. If they do their homework right they will. If it comes down to my design and any of those other guys', credentials could matter.

"I get it, man—you did your undergrad in night classes at a no-name school. You can't change that unless you invest a time-travel machine and redo high school, ace the SAT and win the lottery to pay for college. Get over it. You hide behind that 'I'm not qualified' crap. And it is crap."

JT hated it when Terrance was logical.

"I'm going through the bid materials," he said. "But I'm not sold. We're comfortable, I don't see why you want to risk that."

"Space, JT. Space."

He hung up and walked back to his laptop, where the rough sketch rotated slowly. *Space.* Terrance had all the answers. JT had the doubts. But JT was the one who'd had to fight with everything he had to get where he was. Which meant he had more data than Terrance about how much it would hurt to lose it all over again.

DINNER WITH OLIVIA used to be her oasis. In the early years when she and Cynthia were starting Viva, Hailey had set aside the dinner hour and Olivia's bedtime as sacrosanct. She might have brought work home with her, but she didn't touch it until after she'd sung the last song and turned on Olivia's night-light.

The bedtime routine had fallen by the wayside sometime in middle school, but they'd kept their family dinner hour strong all these years.

These days she and Olivia were still sticking with their nightly ritual, but it was no longer a time when they caught up with each other and shared stories, reconnecting after the day's separation. Now it highlighted that things had gone wrong for their family.

They still split cooking duties the same as they had since the year Olivia turned thirteen. But Olivia had recently settled on a rotation of the dishes she knew her mother hated the most. If Hailey never encountered another eggplant, it would be too soon.

They still met at the kitchen table and still lit the

candles each night, but more often than not, Olivia had bolted her dinner and was sighing impatiently, waiting to be released in less than ten minutes.

They still sat across from each other, radio and TV turned off, but now if Hailey didn't speak, neither did Olivia. Even when she did talk Olivia sometimes ignored her. Hailey spent one night creating a mental catalog of all the many ways Olivia could roll her eyes and what the different variations might mean.

"Molly asked me to sleep over tomorrow," Olivia said.

"Okay."

She was glad Olivia had someone to count on. Her daughter and Molly were almost as close as she and Sarah had been. Hailey hoped Olivia would have the kind of friends that would stick with her through thick and thin.

"Did you and Molly ever become blood sisters?" she blurted. Blurting had become much more common. She sat and thought and stewed and tried to find exactly the words that would unlock the old relationship for them, but eventually something regrettable would just erupt out of her. Inevitably, what she said made the tension much worse than remaining silent would have.

This was one of those times, she thought as Olivia gave her the *my mother is insane* eye roll and said, "No, and if you and Mrs. Finley did that I don't want to know about it."

Hailey felt like rolling her own eyes. She couldn't win.

"Olivia, is there any chance we're going to be able to talk about real things, like what's bothering you? I really miss you."

"Like what's bothering me, Mom? I want to know who my dad is. Anytime you want to talk about that, I'm all ears."

"Why can't you trust me to decide what's best for you?"

"I don't know, Mom. How about because you lied to me about JT all these years?"

Hailey was still trying to figure out something to reply to that when Olivia said, "Mr. McNulty wants me to ask you to come for dinner at his house tomorrow. I'm going to go there and then to Molly's when we're done." She put her plate in the dishwasher and left the room without a backward glance.

It wasn't even an invitation from Olivia, but the fact that her daughter passed it along made her acceptance a no-brainer. If Hailey ever did start wearing slogan T-shirts like Olivia's, she would look for one that read, "Mom = Sucker." She'd go for Olivia. And she'd behave herself around JT. Because she hated the shame she felt when Olivia brought up her lies. If JT knew she'd been with Trevor, the kind of person she'd been when they were together, he'd probably look at her the same way.

"A DINNER PARTY?" JT said.

"Am I speaking English?" Jack had his chair

planted in the middle of the kitchen. JT had been trying to work on his laptop at the table until his dad came in and sprang this on him.

"Tonight?"

"You're catching on. Good job."

"Who would you even invite?" JT had a vision of the parties his mom and dad used to throw when he was a kid. The house would be full of grown-ups, most of them people he knew, but they'd look different dressed up, a lot of them smoking and holding drinks. He and Charlie would be allowed to take a plate upstairs—of appetizers or whatever they could scam from the buffet table. They'd fall asleep much too late, with the sound of shouted laughter and music drifting up to them. "How many people are coming to this thing?"

"What? What people?"

JT closed his laptop and faced his dad. "You said a dinner party. Is it you and me or..."

"You, me, Olivia, Hailey."

Oh.

"I'm...um. Do you know if Hailey...if they want to come?"

"Olivia said she'd bring her."

Which didn't tell JT anything. He knew better than most what Hailey was willing to do for her kid. She'd sure as heck go to a dinner she didn't care about if Olivia wanted her to.

"This is more of your 'making a family for Olivia' thing, right?"

"She likes you."

JT stood and grabbed a glass from the cupboard. "I like her, too. She's a very likable person. But this…dragging me and Hailey into stuff. I asked Hailey to marry me and she said no. I don't even live here anymore."

"You're looking at this wrong. It's not about you and Hailey. It's about Olivia. She wants a family and she got us. Nobody ever said you had to marry her mom."

Well, no, they hadn't. But marrying Hailey wasn't really his current problem, anyway. Kissing her and her kissing back and then…nothing. That was the current problem. Maybe his dad's stupid dinner would shed some light on that situation.

JT turned to lean on the sink. He put the glass down. "Okay. I'll do this for you. But only if you do something for me."

Jack leaned forward. "What?"

"Answer two questions."

"I'll answer one for the party. If you want me to answer the other one, you have to answer one of mine."

"What are we, at the UN?"

"Your choice."

JT shrugged. He had the feeling his questions were going to bug his dad while he…he was an open book. Pretty much.

"Why were you and mom getting a divorce?"

"I spent my life doing what she wanted, being part of her drama. I lost… Let's just say, meeting Olivia made me start thinking differently."

"Why?"

"Is that your second question?"

"No, I guess not."

"Who's Olivia's dad?"

JT snorted and crossed his arms. "What makes you think I know?"

"Answer the question."

"I have no clue. I didn't know she'd cheated on me until she told me she was pregnant. It wasn't a one-time affair, though. I just found that out. I never knew anything."

"None of the kids ever gossiped?" Jack asked.

"I don't think he was a kid." JT had never, not once in his life, shared anything remotely like a secret with his dad. They weren't that kind of family. But for some reason this felt right. Maybe it was that Jack was asking because he cared about Olivia, not because he was hoping to tear Hailey down.

"I think it was an older guy and he scared her somehow. Otherwise, why would she ask me to lie? Her parents hated me, you know? I wouldn't have been anyone's top pick as a son-in-law back then. So if it was another kid, why not say that?"

Jack had turned away during his explanation, but now faced JT, deliberately meeting his eyes. "I'm sorry for the way I let her folks treat you. What you did for Hailey. I don't think it was a good choice, but I can see why you did it, and it took guts. You shouldered the heat from all of us and never said a word."

Now JT looked away. He and Jack just didn't say stuff like that to each other.

He managed to mumble, "Thanks."

"You have any guesses about the guy?" Jack said.

"She totally fooled me, Dad. In case you haven't noticed she's an effective liar." JT shrugged. "Doesn't really matter, though."

"It matters to Olivia." Jack shifted in his chair. "You have one more question coming."

JT nodded, happy to leave the subject of Hailey. "Right. Okay." He took a deep breath. "Why won't you do your therapy? Don't you want to get better?"

Jack opened his mouth and JT saw it coming. His dad had shut down so many conversations over the past couple weeks—he was going to drop some insult and that would be it. But then his expression changed and he clenched his jaw before saying, "It's not about wanting to get better. I just... Nothing works. My whole life I had my strength. The garage, football before that, hell, even your mom—everything I ever did or won, it was with my body. And now I can't stop shaking when all I'm doing is trying to stand up. It's humiliating. It's too much."

JT didn't know what to say. Of all the reasons he'd thought Jack might give, this wasn't what he'd expected. Hailey was right, his dad was afraid. JT almost couldn't take it in. "Therapy will help with that. Hailey said she can help."

"I know. I'm working on it." Jack pushed his

wheelchair forward and back restlessly. "About the dinner, you can order food from somewhere. Just make sure you get something a kid would like."

Most times when his dad cut the conversation short, his last words were bitter or rude or actually mean. But this time, as he left, JT felt his dad's sadness and his fear. His world had been turned inside out and he was trying to do something to put it back together. He screwed up a lot, no one would deny that. But he literally had no clue how to be the guy he was trying to be. JT wondered if Olivia had any idea about the effect she was having on his dad's life. He didn't guess she did. But JT figured he could at least make sure this dinner went the way she and Jack would like.

HE'D SET UP an old card table on the porch and covered it with a tablecloth he found in the linen closet. There was a cooler by the back door stocked with lemonade, root beer, sparkling water and a few bottles of beer for the adults. He'd run a speaker wire out through the kitchen window that afternoon and, while his dad sat at the kitchen table, had downloaded a few dozen top-forty songs to his iPod. Jack's disgust at the type of music had entertained JT way more than it would have when he was a teenager. So now they were eating with the dulcet tones of the All-American Rejects flowing through the speakers.

The setup had gone well, JT figured, but he'd really outdone himself with the dinner.

"What are you going to do with all the left-overs?" Hailey asked as she chose from the second card table, where he'd laid out a buffet of fried chicken, corn on the cob, applesauce, a pan of corn bread, two kinds of potato salad, coleslaw, fruit salad and a three-tier tray of what the lady at the bakery had called "Dessert for Twelve."

"Charlie will eat it," JT said. "For a rich guy he doesn't seem to be much of a grocery shopper."

"I'm having seconds on dessert," Olivia stated. "Don't give it away yet."

"I told you this was the way to go." JT nudged his dad. "He wanted me to cook."

"That's an outright lie." Jack laughed. "We'd have been eating scrambled eggs and toast, and there's only so much of that a man can take."

"Is that still the only thing you can cook?" Hailey leaned back in her chair. "Remember you made me scrambled eggs the morning after the prom?"

Olivia's mouth dropped open. "Grandma let you stay out all night after the prom?"

"She thought I was at Sarah's," Hailey admitted.

"Is JT a good dancer?"

JT stood up. "That's my cue to get myself another brownie."

"He was an enthusiastic dancer," Hailey said. "You should have seen him when he was in the Bulldog costume."

"Wait," Olivia said. "You were the Bulldog?"

JT pulled his chair away from the table and

turned it so when he sat again he was facing out into the yard, where the last fingers of orange and pink from the sunset were still visible over the garage roof.

"Charlie was this phenomenal football player, you know? So my senior year, he was a sophomore and he got the starting quarterback job. Everyone said the team was going to state and I really wanted to be there." He bit into his brownie. "I wasn't about to try out for football, but the mascot travels with the team. So, yeah, I was the Bulldog."

"That must have been awesome."

"It was hot more than anything. And the Bulldog head is heavy. Hurt my neck every game."

"Don't listen to him," Hailey said. "He was so much fun. He could get the whole stadium going, doing these ridiculous chants."

"Remember when I got the student section to moon that team from Alysetown?"

"You almost got suspended for that," Jack interjected. "I had to go down and talk Father Gregory into letting you off with a month of detention."

"The good old days," JT said.

"Your brother never got suspended, not once. It was always you."

"Did you go to state?" Olivia's attempt to distract Jack wasn't subtle, but it was effective.

JT smiled at her. "Ask Charlie to show you his ring sometime. I'd show you mine but they don't give a ring to the Bulldog."

Olivia tipped her lemonade bottle up and drained

it. "This was really nice, Mr. McNulty. Thanks. And thanks, JT. But Molly's expecting me. I should go."

JT barely even noticed when she hugged Jack—what would have been so strange a few weeks ago now seemed perfectly normal. When she hugged him, he hugged her back. "Thanks," he whispered, even though she would have no idea what he was thanking her for.

Jack wheeled himself over to the buffet and grabbed a paper plate. "Take some of the dessert with you, okay?"

Hailey dug her keys out of her purse while Jack and Olivia filled a plate. "This was really nice, JT," she said.

"Yeah. It was."

CHAPTER TEN

AFTER DROPPING OLIVIA OFF, Hailey drove home alone. Sarah was on the patio, sitting with her feet tucked under her on a chair pulled up close to the fireplace.

"That looks wonderful," Hailey said. "Mind if I join you?"

Sarah pushed a chair toward her with one foot. "Grab a seat."

"Where are the kids?" she asked.

"Inside. They had a screaming fight so I made them go to their rooms. Simon fell asleep but Lily's still up. Probably plotting my death."

Hailey pulled her chair closer to the fire. "This is really nice."

"I never made my own fire before," Sarah said. "Isn't that stupid? We have this gorgeous patio out here and we rarely have fires because Erik isn't here and I always left this to him."

"It's a great fire," Hailey said.

Sarah sighed. "You know what? Men make it seem like building a fire is this big, mysterious chore that you have to like, take man lessons in before you can ever do it right."

"Man lessons?"

"It's not true. If you want a fire, you pile up some wood and you light a match. Presto—fire."

Hailey laughed. "So you have a new skill. Congratulations."

"And one less reason to need Erik."

Hailey frowned. "Do you want to talk about him?"

Sarah leaned down and picked up a length of firewood from the pile on the ground near her chair. She poked it into the fireplace and watched the flames for a moment. "No, I don't. I am enjoying myself with my fire and I don't want to wreck that. As a matter of fact, I think I'm owed some vicarious living. How's JT?"

"Good, I think. We had dinner."

"Dinner?"

"With Jack and Olivia. But he was sweet. He and Jack are both so nice to Olivia."

"I thought there was going to be more vicarious kissing," Sarah complained.

"Debby said something hateful about him."

"Debby? Sweet Debby, your receptionist?" Sarah asked. "What does she have against JT?"

"She doesn't like the way he abandoned Olivia."

"Huh."

"All this time I was thinking about the lie and what it meant for Olivia and for me, but I didn't really think about him. I mean, I thought about him and Olivia, but not *him.* I set him up as her father, but then when he asked to be her father for real I turned him down."

"He was just a kid and not a super responsible one," Sarah said. "That wasn't necessarily a bad decision."

"I did it because I didn't love him. After Trevor, I knew I couldn't be with someone I didn't love."

"He loved you, though. That was obvious."

"He didn't even know me. He only loved what he thought I was."

Sarah used the poker to stir the logs, sending sparks shooting up into the night. "So where are you going with this?"

"I just wonder. When we kissed the other night. Was he kissing me or was he kissing his old girlfriend?"

"Only one way to find out."

Hailey stood to go. "I'm not sure I want to know."

"Well, if you find out, remember you owe me some vicarious kissing."

Hailey crossed the dark driveway and went into her quiet house. With Olivia gone for the night, the silence felt empty. It was a relief after the angry silence that had been their constant companion recently.

JT had been so funny tonight, engaging his dad and Olivia, letting them make fun of his atomic watch and letting her tell the story about the Bulldog. He'd changed in so many ways, but was still so much the same.

She wondered what it would be like to kiss him again. Would he want to? If he did, if she had him come here, to her home, would she be able to strip back her defenses and let him get to know her? Would he be able to see past her exterior and would he even want to know the woman she was?

Hailey picked up the phone before she could think about it again, and quickly dialed his number.

He answered on the first ring. "Hailey?"

"Olivia went out."

"I know."

She was quiet, not sure exactly what she wanted, but unwilling to hang up.

"Did you call just to tell me that?"

"Is your dad okay?"

"Sleeping."

Another silence.

"Hailey?"

"I had a really good time kissing you and I wondered if you might want to come over and do it some more."

She thought he might have dropped the phone. Or hung up. The silence stretched on.

"The last time we did that it didn't work out so well."

"I've done some thinking since then. I'm not promising…well…anything. Except more kissing. If you want to."

"Okay."

He didn't sound sure. Had she just made a horrible fool of herself?

"I'm sorry. You don't have to..." She was pretty sure she heard a car door slam on his end of the line and then an engine turning over. "Are you in your car?"

"Faster than walking. Where do you live exactly?"

Hailey told him the address, while smiling so wide she felt it in her scalp.

"I'm on my way."

"Good," she said. She went outside to wait for him, her stomach skipping with anticipation.

"CHARLIE? I NEED YOU TO run to the house and spend the night with Dad."

"Why?"

"Personal stuff," he said. "But there's a ton of food there. You can have a field day. And Dad's asleep."

Charlie must have heard something in his voice. Maybe JT had even made sure there was something in his voice for Charlie to hear. He wanted to tell someone, to see if he was making a stupid fool of himself.

"You're not going to Hailey's," his brother said. "Don't do this to yourself."

Turned out he didn't much care if Charlie thought he was making a stupid fool of himself.

"Will you sit with Dad or not?"

"Yes. But I'm advising you strongly against this course of action." His brother's business voice was rife with authority, but didn't make a dent in JT's excitement.

"Here's the thing, Charlie. She's the one."

"The one?"

"Yeah, you know. The *one.*"

"The one? The only one for you, the one? You love her?" Charlie sounded bewildered and a little disgusted.

"God, Charlie. You're like the sister I never had," JT said. "Not that one. The one I never slept with."

"Oh."

"Now you got nothing to say?"

"I thought you slept with her. You went out with her for almost a whole year."

"Didn't happen."

"Not even once?"

"Charlie, please. I think I'd notice if we'd had sex."

"So this whole time you took the rap for knocking her up and you never even got to sleep with her?"

Charlie sounded so put out about that, the least important part of what had happened, that JT had to laugh. Trust his brother to be concerned with equity, he was the only kid JT had ever known who'd dreamed of being a ref in the NFL instead of on a team.

"I guess I can sit with Dad if it means you get to be with your one," Charlie said. "Let me know if you need me."

There was a pause and then JT said, "I don't even want to know what you think I might need you for. Sicko."

JT closed his phone and held it for a second. He understood what Charlie had been trying to tell him. But the trouble was, he wasn't Charlie. His brother would never know what Hailey had meant to him.

That period right after she'd told him she wouldn't marry him had been the worst time of his life. Her rejection had seemed to validate everything his parents had said. He was too young, too stupid, too foolish, too everything to be worth anything to anyone.

He still wasn't sure about her. The lie and the way she'd used him continued to be raw spots. But everything else was, well, was Hailey. He couldn't figure out how to reconcile the person who'd cheated on him, lied to her parents and then used his name without his permission to lie to her child all those years. But he wanted to think she'd have a reason. Because the Hailey he knew wouldn't have done that so there must be a reason.

Sarah Finley's Tudor house was set back on a large lot. A driveway snaked up the side of the property and disappeared behind the house. JT drove up and parked on the side behind Hailey's Mustang.

He smelled a pool and heard the gentle sound of the water moving through the filter before he saw her, standing in the doorway of the carriage house. He raised a hand and she waved back. She was still wearing the silky skirt she'd had on at dinner. It showed off her gorgeous legs to perfection. The light shining over her shoulder made her skin glow, even though he couldn't make out her expression.

She came out to meet him on the gravel driveway and his heart was thumping loud in his chest. He couldn't believe she'd called him. She was so familiar to him but different, too. The years had been good to Hailey. A few extra pounds in just the right places made her sexier than she'd been when she was younger.

"Hi," she murmured as she stepped closer to put her arms around his neck. "I really had fun doing this the other night."

The water lapping against the sides of the pool made a counterpoint to the blood pounding through his veins. It wasn't as if he'd been a monk in the years since he'd been in school, but the other night, when they'd been making out like a pair of teenagers, he'd been shocked to find he was having trouble controlling himself.

Now he was back in the same uncomfortable condition, holding Hailey, doing everything he could to hang on to his self-control.

They moved backward across the driveway, toward the carriage house.

"JT," she murmured between kisses. "I want…"

"Want what?" he asked, not really paying attention. He would have paid attention if she hadn't tasted so good, if she hadn't—

"Want to sleep together?"

He dropped his hands. "What?"

"Would you? Can we make love?"

"Now? Here?" He'd talked a good game to Charlie, but he'd really never thought they'd have sex tonight. He'd have been happy to go on kissing her for a good long time. "What?"

"I want to have sex with you. Tonight."

Huh. She actually *had* said that.

She was flushed, her lips parted, her hands held out from her sides slightly. She opened herself to him, even as she said she wanted to make love.

He took her hands and then smoothed his up her bare arms to hold her shoulders lightly. "You don't have to say that. I'm okay with this." He bent to her lips again.

She ducked her head away from him and he wondered for a second if she was hiding tears. But that made no sense, and when she looked back at him, her eyes were bright but clear.

"Please."

He pulled her close, wanting contact with her, as much contact as he could get. "You got it, Hailey. If you want this, you got it."

"Okay. I want it."

Which really was an invitation he couldn't refuse. On the bench in the freaking rehab center, Hailey, in all her clothes, had about driven him over the edge. To finally see what had been hiding under Hailey's perfect wardrobe all these years? He'd never gotten that far with her. Never even seen her bra. She'd been so clear about the limits.

But all that was about to change. How many guys ever got to do this? Have their fantasy night with their fantasy girl? He'd imagined this so many times, Hailey's perfect body in some perfect scrap of satin. He shuddered just thinking about it, and pushed her gently to get her moving toward the house. She put her hand on the doorknob and then licked her lips. She smoothed a finger across those lips, spreading the moisture.

When she raised her finger to his lips, he nipped it, pulling it into his mouth and sucking. He wrapped his arm around her waist and pulled her to him, thrilled at the way her body felt against his. She still had one hand on the doorknob, and the way her body was angled backward left her throat and her breast open to him.

Almost open to him. Soon. *God.*

"Let me in, Hailey. Before I embarrass myself."

She colored and pulled him all the way inside. He loved that she blushed. He'd rattled the impeccable composure of Hailey Maddox. He tightened his grip on her waist and almost groaned her name, strangled by the heat and weight of his need.

He put his other hand on her waist and turned them so he could back through the room, drawing her after him. The living room was lit by one tabletop lamp, the light from the patio adding to the dim glow and creating odd, fractured shadows through the slats of the wooden blinds.

He bent his head and their mouths met. He'd never been this hungry for a kiss, a touch. But Hailey was right there to meet him, her mouth open to receive, demanding more and more.

If she wanted more, he was happy to oblige.

"Hailey," he mumbled against her mouth as he cupped her neck with one hand, the other running hard down the front of her sweater. Her breasts were perfect. "Hailey, I can't do this the way I should. I just… I've wanted…so long…."

"You talk too much," she answered, and then she licked his mouth, catching him off guard. She leaned back to grin at him. "I didn't ask you over here to talk."

Oh, God, JT thought as he lowered his head to her neck. He nuzzled in under her hair behind her ear as he moved his hands down to her ass. She had a great ass. Killer. He loved the way it filled his hands, and he knew, just knew, that when he finally saw her without all these clothes, it was going to have been worth the wait.

She arched her hips into him, their bodies fitting so tight, his erection pressing against her with exquisite perfection. He couldn't stand it. Quicker than he'd have imagined possible, he had the buttons of her sweater undone and then her shirt, and he was peeling it back, his eyes and hands and mouth hungry for her.

"Huh," he said as he stopped.

Hailey pressed against him. Why was he stopping? He'd been giving her exactly what she needed, more than she'd hoped for but the merest taste of what she was willing to take. And then he'd stopped.

She felt his hand up under her skirt, but he wasn't

touching her the way he had been, like a man intent on discovering the hidden pleasures of a woman's body. This was more like he was rummaging under the hood, checking for a loose fan belt.

Then he lifted the side of her skirt and bent to look under it exactly the way he might if he were lifting a bed skirt to locate a missing sock, and said, "Huh" again. She lost her patience.

"Huh, what?" she asked as she twitched her skirt out of his hand and pressed it back down. "Is this some new technique the girls in Pittsburgh like?"

"No. I, just… What are you wearing?" He seemed genuinely puzzled. Puzzled on JT was normally adorable, the way his nose crinkled. But now? In this moment? Adorable wasn't what she was looking for.

"What do you mean, what am I wearing?" she snapped.

He poked her white cotton bra with one finger. "This. What's this?" And then he reached under her skirt again, hooked a finger in the leg of her underpants and tugged. "And this."

"My underwear?" He'd lost her. And she was quickly losing the heat she'd spent the past ten minutes cultivating. Which was making her short-tempered.

He closed his eyes wearily and said, "That's it. That's the problem."

"What problem?"

"Hailey, you…" He paused to cup her breasts and breathe in deeply, his face inches from her skin.

His touch now was firm and possessive, exactly what she wanted. She moved against his hands in encouragement and he took the hint, pressing his hips into hers and sliding his thumbs under the cups of her bra to rub her nipples with the most perfect, most amazing pressure. "You can't call it underwear. And it should be silky and much smaller."

"Smaller?"

"Yes, because you're very sexy, Hailey. Like off-the-charts sexy. Like record-book, all-time *Sports Illustrated Swimsuit Issue* sexy." He put both hands on her right breast and dipped his head and then, with his hands full of her, he mumbled, "You're perfect. Your underwear is messing that up."

She couldn't breathe. His lips were more than she could handle. She reached desperately for his zipper. She needed him.

"I'm not perfect," she managed to pant. "Stop saying that."

"Yes, Hailey, you are. You always have been."

He was ruining it. He was supposed to see her. The real her. And he was so close. He saw her, but he was trying to take who she really was and stuff it back into the image he had in his mind.

She took his face in her hands and made him focus on her. "I'm not perfect. I'm just me. Can't we be together like this, as we really are? Please?"

His eyes were wide with passion and she knew he didn't understand what she was asking. But he nodded and kissed the inside of her wrist. A shiver ran up her arm.

"No more talking." She pulled his head back down toward her breast. "Stop stopping. Keep touching."

He set to work then in a most satisfyingly single-minded way, making sure every part of her body understood exactly what he meant by sexy. She was so high she didn't think she'd ever be back down. She'd never been with anyone who could communicate with his hands exactly what he was thinking. And she definitely liked what JT was thinking.

Hailey found the button on his jeans and the zipper, and pulled them down. She plunged her hand inside and felt him straining against his boxer briefs.

"Can I?" she asked, but then didn't wait for his answer, threading her hands in the waistband and pushing both his boxers and pants down. He toed out of his shoes and then stepped out of the jeans. He pulled his shirt off over his head, his shoulders and back flexing as he dragged the T-shirt up and off.

JT had grown up, was the first inane thought that went through her mind. After that, after her swift and vivid inventory of smoothly muscled shoulders, pecs and abs, tapered waist, slim hips, she stopped seeing and thinking and let herself feel.

He peeled her skirt and underwear off and then slid her blouse off her arms. He popped her bra and removed it, and then they were naked together, the slatted shadows throwing their bodies into strange patterns of light and dark.

He wrapped his arms around her, almost gently then, sliding his hands in one delicious, shivering line from her shoulders to her hips and then between her legs. She moved against his hand, and that was all it took. She couldn't have described what it was like, their excitement perfectly balanced, their rhythm matched and thrilling. She moved them toward her bedroom, finally pulling him down with her onto the bed. He said her name once and she knew what he wanted, what he was asking. She tugged him to her but he cursed and kissed her hard on the lips and then, moving down her body, kissed her quick on the stomach, the top of her thigh, her knee, and finally hard again on her instep, before rolling off the bed.

"Don't move."

He was back in a heartbeat, a condom in his hand, and she smiled and reached for him. He was trembling, little quivers running across his shoulders under her fingers. But he took the time to make sure she was ready for him, and when he finally pushed inside her she was just as eager as he was.

Her whole body was full with the strength of him and the strength of how he made her feel. She rocked against him as he apologized for not being able to hold on, but he slid a hand between them and it turned out she couldn't hold on, either. She came just after he did, both of them collapsing against each other.

When their breathing had evened out, when she could think something besides just *JT,* she raised her head and said, "So, what? The girls in Pittsburgh all wear thongs?"

A lazy teasing smile drifted across his face as he nodded, and she kissed the corner of his mouth, loving that she could do that. That he was here in her bed and if she wanted to kiss the grin right off his face she could. Except she wouldn't. Because JT's grin was a very nice part of him.

"Sometimes they don't wear anything at all."

"JT!" She slapped his shoulder.

"Hey. Play nice." He ran a hand down her side, curling his fingers into her hip in a way that made her yearn toward him. "Here's the deal. I waited fifteen years to make love to you. Then tonight, I worked pretty darn hard to get into your clothes…"

"I called you."

"I made that whole dinner."

"First of all, you bought the dinner. Second of all, *I* said, 'Will you make love to me?'"

"No more contradicting," he said. "I'm explaining something to you. My point is, a guy wants a payoff. Once you work and get through the preliminaries and you're starting the main event—"

"The main event?" She couldn't stifle the laugh. He was so serious about whatever he was telling her.

"Be quiet. After all that build up, a guy expects silk or lace or something that makes you go uh-hmm."

He nuzzled her neck with a deep appreciative sound and she shivered.

"You said huh, not uh-hmm."

"Exactly. Your underwear is too big."

"I like my underwear. I like the cotton. I like to be covered up."

He met her eyes, his face serious. "I didn't mean to insult you. I was just surprised. You're always so—"

"Don't you dare say perfect."

"How about well-dressed?"

"But isn't this, part of what we're doing, aren't we getting to know each other? Aren't there parts of you I'd be surprised by? Can't there be parts of me that aren't what you expect?"

"Oh, goddamn, Hailey, you look like that and I start to think I could have fantasies about big cotton underwear. Wear whatever you like."

Which hadn't really been her point. She decided to let it go. He was here now. That counted for something.

"But you really think I should go buy new underwear."

"Call them panties," he murmured. She could feel his smile against the skin of her shoulder as he kissed her.

"Silk underwear?" She rubbed against him when she said "silk." Imagined that she was wearing just a tiny scrap of silk, and what it would feel like to be with him in nothing but that.

He put his arm around her and tucked her in close. "Nope. You're doing fine on your own. No need for overkill."

"But if I did have them, you would find that sexier?"

"Hailey, I don't know if I could stand it if I found you any sexier."

"I think I want to try it."

"I think I've created a monster."

"What if I just skipped it altogether? Like those girls in Pittsburgh? That would be sexy to you?"

"Oh, God." JT moaned. But she felt him hardening again, and loved that it was because of her. She turned to face him, and kissed his chest. This what-if was definitely a yes, at least for tonight.

WHEN THEY WERE FINALLY finished, or at least, finally exhausted, he pulled Hailey close and lay with her head resting on his shoulder.

Hailey traced a slow circle on his chest with her fingertip. "Our lives are so different now. Remember you used to be so mad about your curfew?"

"Yeah. But I was too afraid my dad would kick my ass if I ever broke it."

She smiled. "He wouldn't have."

"Probably not. He was so unpredictable, kept me guessing."

"Are you glad you came home?"

"When I first saw your underwear, as you like to call them, I wasn't so sure. But I think I can deal."

She pinched him and then, when he seemed to like that, she bit him. But *she* liked *that*, and thought about mustering the energy to crawl back on top of him and bite and pinch him some more.

He stroked her hair, and she surrendered to the pleasure of being held and muscle-quivering exhaustion.

"Believe me, Hailey," he said. "The spirit is willing, but the flesh is weak."

"I wasn't talking about this, anyway. I meant your dad and…and everything." She almost said "and me" but she lost her nerve.

"I'm glad. I'm not sure anyone would understand it, but I am."

"Can you stay here tonight?"

JT patted her shoulder. "Hailey, there is no way I'd willingly leave your bed to go back home to Jack. Charlie's there. I'm good."

She hadn't shared a bed with a man in years. The last time had been at a cousin's wedding when she and the groom's best friend from high school had struck up a quick relationship over too many rum and cokes. But with JT next to her, Hailey lay awake for a few minutes and savored the way he changed her bedroom. She liked listening to him breathe. The feel of his strong body next to hers was comforting and exciting. She was going to fall asleep and when she woke up he'd still be there.

JT WOKE UP BEFORE Hailey. She was turned away from him, but her back and her butt and her feet were all curled backwards, pressing against him. He liked that feeling. Liked it a lot.

He hadn't gotten much of a sense of her room the night before. It suited her, he decided. The walls were painted with one of those faux-finish techniques that used about six layers of paint to produce a rich, warm, pale-orange-and-cream glow. He'd dated a woman one time who'd sponge-painted her living room, so he knew how wrong this kind of work could go. It made sense to him that Hailey would do it right. It was just the kind of meticulous job he thought suited her attention to detail.

Detail. That was a good word for this room. There was no clutter; the top of the low chest under the window was perfectly clear and the upholstered chair in the corner was empty, too. He knew if that chair was in his bedroom it would be piled with three weeks' worth of unfolded laundry.

Pictures of Olivia as a baby and young girl were framed in mismatched but coordinated gold wood frames, heavy on the floral carving. It was an old-fashioned effect but appealing. The whole place was appealing, including Hailey, who was beginning to stir next to him.

"Hey," he said softly.

"Mmm," she answered, and rolled toward him.

That was really all the persuading either of them needed to revisit some of the high points from the night before and to discover some entirely new, wonderfully satisfying endeavors.

CHAPTER ELEVEN

"I HAVE GOT TO GO," JT said reluctantly the next morning. "Charlie has work."

"What about *your* work?" Hailey asked. "Don't you need to go back?"

He sighed. "I have a partner. He can hold down the fort for a while yet."

"Have you been in Pittsburgh all this time? Is that where you went when you left?"

"Yeah. I was supposed to go to Vermont, remember? But my dad wouldn't give me my college money."

"But you earned that money."

He had. He'd started working in the garage when he was ten, but his dad never paid him. Instead he gave JT a tally book and they kept a record in there of what he would have earned. The money was supposed to be his when he went to college.

"They were so mad about everything, they wouldn't let me have it. I'm not resentful anymore. And anyway, it all worked out. I went to Pittsburgh. I knew a couple of guys who'd gone out there for school and I moved in with them. I got a job in the campus facilities garage at Carnegie Mellon. One day this guy came in, wanted to know if we had a solder gun he could use. Said the one in his lab burned out and he was on a deadline. My boss told me to show him the stuff, but watch him. He didn't trust the academics—they were notorious for screwing up the tools."

JT rubbed his hand down her side while he talked. She stretched into it and he curled his fingers around her hip. "I hit it off with the guy, Terrance, and we ended up going back to the lab he was working in after we fixed his part. I'd never seen anything like that lab. The stuff they were doing—it blew my mind away."

"Terrance is your partner?"

JT nodded. "We kept in touch. Played on a Frisbee team together. He convinced me to enroll in night school and tutored me. When I graduated he talked the professor running his lab into writing a recommendation for me and I got into Carnegie Mellon for grad school. Terrance started RoboGen and I joined him as soon as I finished."

"I don't want you to take this the wrong way, JT, but that's an amazing story."

"Luck mostly."

"I doubt that. When you left here you'd just been voted Most Likely to be Expelled the Day Before Graduation. You weren't exactly on the path to supergeek."

"Sometimes you find the right fit."

She moved her leg over his. "Like this."

"Yep." He raised her hand to his lips and kissed it. "Like this."

"Why didn't you ever come home?"

"My folks and I said some awful things.... And my feelings were hurt. I mean, I offered to marry you."

She raised her head. "But you didn't know what you were offering. You just did that to be nice."

He jerked backward. "No. I did it because I wanted to marry you."

"You didn't even know me."

"You keep saying that, but it's not true. What didn't I know?"

She was stung by that statement. Angry. He hadn't known anything. She'd been trying to explain this to him and he wasn't getting it.

"That I'd been cheating on you for months. That I was sneaking off with someone else, doing things I wouldn't do with you." That hurt him, she saw.

"Besides that."

"What I wanted, what my hopes were, who I really was."

He was still. Quiet. Even his breathing seemed to slow down. Then he slid gently out from under her. He sat on the edge of the bed with his back to her.

"If I didn't know you it's because you didn't let me," he said. "Same as I can't know you now if you're going to continue keeping everything secret."

"I'm not going to tell you who Olivia's father is just so you can feel better about sleeping with me."

He shook his head. "That's not what I mean, as

you're well aware. You want me to understand you. You don't want me to see you as perfect. But that's all you show me. You're covering up, and keeping your secrets is taking so much energy, there's no way anybody can get close to you."

"I can't."

He pulled his jeans on and stood next to the bed as he zipped and buttoned them. She watched his hands move, strong and sure, and her body ached because he wouldn't be touching her again.

"I'm not going to tell you what to do. It's your decision. But I can't ever do what you want—know you for real—until you start letting yourself be real. And you can't do that while you're lying about Olivia's dad. You're killing every chance you have with Olivia, any chance we might have. Is it worth it?"

He pulled his shirt on over his head and tucked it into his pants. "I walked away from my folks, Hailey. In two years Olivia will be exactly the age I was. You don't have a heck of a lot of time with her. You and me, we might be out of time already."

She watched him walk out of the bedroom before she sank back into the pillows and let the tears come. She'd tried. She'd brought him here, made love to him, been as genuine as she could, and it hadn't been enough. He was right. Sticking with Trevor's rules was killing her. She just wasn't sure it wouldn't kill Olivia if the truth came out.

JT SNAPPED AT CHARLIE when he made a joke about "the one," and his brother told him to grow up. He went upstairs to shower before Jack could say anything to him.

As he stood under the water, he leaned his head on the tile wall. He should never have said those things. He had no right to push Hailey. No right to expect her to do anything or be anything different than what she was.

He wasn't planning to stay here, anyway. Why couldn't he just have kept his mouth shut and enjoyed himself for a couple more weeks? He didn't need to push. Shouldn't have let her know he wanted something more.

He'd been stupid again and he knew it was going to go badly.

HAILEY ARRIVED ON TIME for the therapy session with his dad later that morning. JT let her in, but she acted as if he was merely an acquaintance. Jack was right there, too, so it was possible she was just trying to be professional, but JT didn't think so. He'd screwed things up with her. He should have kept his mouth shut about that stupid lie.

He went to sit on the back porch so he wouldn't be tempted to shove his way into his dad's room and demand to talk to her. He was flipping his Frisbee from one hand to the next when Olivia came around the corner of the house. Her T-shirt today was yellow and printed with a police officers badge that read, "Gravity. It's the Law." He'd started to look forward to her shirts.

"How come you're out here?" she asked.

"Your mom's here," he said. "I'm giving them privacy."

"Your dad likes to make a fuss about stuff, doesn't he?"

JT nodded.

"Most times he doesn't mean it, though."

She knew his dad, that was for sure.

She watched him flip the Frisbee a few more times. "Could you show me how to throw that?"

"The Frisbee?"

She nodded.

"Back up," he said. He moved to a spot a few yards away from her. "It's your wrist mainly. You need to snap it."

He flicked the disc to her and she caught it neatly.

She turned it in her hand, trying to get a comfortable hold. He had the idea she wasn't really looking at it, though. As a matter of fact, he was pretty sure she'd come out here on purpose to ask him something, and the Frisbee was her cover. She seemed unsure of how to proceed. "You need anything?" he asked.

"Do you know who my dad is?" Flat out. No messing around, which was surprising, because Olivia wasn't much for telling anyone what she really thought. Not that she was sneaky, but she was self-contained, happy enough to join a conversation and with a very quick mind. But she didn't offer details about herself or her feelings.

He thought about telling her she needed to ask

her mother, but that wouldn't help anyone. And besides, if she was starting to ask people, the best thing he could do was tell her the truth. If she thought there was an answer to be found she'd keep pushing and possibly get hurt, but if she knew the truth she might let it ride until Hailey was ready to tell her. If Hailey ever got to that point.

"I don't, Olivia."

She watched him as he answered and he gazed straight at her, willing her to believe him.

"Would you lie to me?"

"Not about this." She still didn't appear convinced. "Look, if I did know who he was and I knew your mom didn't want you to know, which it's pretty clear she doesn't, I wouldn't tell you. It's not my place. But I would tell you to ask your mother. I wouldn't lie. I'm not lying now. I have no idea. And believe me, I've put some thought into the issue."

"He was married. Were you aware of that?"

"No, no, I wasn't," he said slowly. He guessed it made sense but it wasn't something he wanted to think about. He'd seen what an affair did to his parents' marriage. Hailey must have been so messed up.

"Why did you lie about being my dad?" She tossed the Frisbee toward him. It wobbled but he managed to catch it.

"More snap," he said as he sent it back to her.

JT wished with everything he had that he'd never gotten started on this conversation. This girl with her sad eyes and her sad questions and the way she wanted something from somebody was going to kill him.

"I lied because your mom asked me to," he said. "She needed help and I…" He almost said, "I loved her" but that wasn't something he should tell Hailey's daughter. So instead he repeated, "She asked me to."

"You know what's funny?" Olivia asked. He shook his head, unwilling to even guess. "I waited all this time to meet you because I thought you were my dad, but I kind of hated you. Because, you know, you never showed up."

Her throw this time was sharper. He wondered if she was getting the hang of it or if her anger had given it an edge.

He caught the Frisbee, flinching as he did. Damn it, this sucked. Still, if Olivia had something to say and she was brave enough, he owed her the space to say it. He hadn't knowingly hurt her, but neither had he spared a thought for her all these years. She hadn't been a person to him, just Hailey's baby.

"So then I met you and you're not my dad, so I don't hate you and I don't have to like you, but I do. If my mom did have random sex with some schmuck who abandoned us and then showed up when I was almost too old to need a dad, I hope he'd be as cool as you."

Right before he made a joke JT realized his mouth was dry. He threw the Frisbee to her and she caught it again. Goddamn it, this kid was something. It wasn't as if he hadn't thought about it, seeing her with his dad, with Hailey, around the house. What it would have been like, if Hailey had picked him. The way it looked to him, he'd been the one who missed out. "You're a good kid, Olivia. I'd be proud to be your dad."

He hoped they were finished. Not quite. She looked away from him, holding the Frisbee against her leg.

"I wish I knew who the schmuck really was. Who could be so bad she won't tell me? That's the part that bugs me. Somebody out there gave me half my DNA and I don't get to know it. Like, what if I'm just like him and I'm pre-schmucky and I don't know so I can't stop myself? But if I knew what was wrong with him then I could stop from becoming that."

JT wanted to give her a hug, but didn't know if he should and wasn't sure she would have wanted it, anyway. But she was so damn worried and sort of lost, and it was just wrong. Ever since she'd first showed up, he'd been thanking God she was there for Jack. She made his dad happy for some reason, and that made *his* life a whole hell of a lot easier.

But for the first time, he was glad Jack was in her life for her. He'd seen them together and knew that whatever metamorphosis his dad was going through, Olivia was the one who got the best of it. So maybe his father, who'd never had much time for anybody but his wife, would be the one who'd be there for this kid. If it couldn't be JT, he was glad it was his dad.

"The only person you're like is you, kid. You're

not a schmuck. Not even pre-schmucky. I say, go along and live your life, and if you meet the guy someday, remember your mom was a kid and you gotta give her a break."

Olivia took in a breath, almost as if she were breathing his words in and holding them inside. Then she ducked her head, swallowing. He couldn't see her face when she muttered, "Thanks."

He hoped he'd helped her, reassured her, at least for today. The issues she was dealing with weren't going to get fixed anytime soon, so he figured if she made it through one day at a time keeping her self-esteem intact then she'd eventually come out the other side okay.

After they'd been silent for a few seconds, she tilted her head and wrinkled her nose. She snapped her wrist and the throw was perfect this time. "It's weird that you still love her. I mean, she cheated on you and she won't tell you who he is, either. But you love her."

And then she walked past him into the house.

JT dropped onto the bottom step. *Holy crap.* Was that what it was like to be a dad? He'd been through a lot in his lifetime, but he was wrung out from what must have been a four-minute conversation. He didn't envy anyone who had to do that on a regular basis. But then he remembered the tentative smile Olivia had given him and how she took his reassurance in as if she were going to hold on to it, and he knew it wouldn't be the worst thing in the world if someone wanted to give him a chance to be a dad for real.

JACK HAD STARTED the session badly. He wouldn't pay attention. Pretended he didn't understand her instructions and basically pulled all kinds of tricks to waste time, use up their appointment before he did any of the work.

Hailey wondered if he thought she didn't notice.

He wouldn't look at her. She'd seen that before—in men mostly, sometimes in female athletes. They got so used to their bodies doing what they needed that the injuries were an insult, a deep, terrifying crack in who they were. It was as if once one thing had gone wrong, they all of a sudden started imagining what else could go wrong.

"Time out."

Jack stopped the lifts, but didn't relax his grip on the arms of his wheelchair.

"I've been letting you slide, but you're not paying me to babysit."

"I've been trying to work. You're the one who asked for a time out."

"I want you to think about what you're giving up every day you let yourself be scared off working the right way."

"I'm not—"

"You are. And that's normal. But it's time to deal with it. You're not going to come back one hundred percent the way you were before. But you have every right to expect that you can get a heck of a lot closer than you are now. Except, you have to work for it. You're going to look foolish and you're going to have bad days, but none of that means anything if you come out the other side on your own two feet."

Jack's grip on the chair loosened and his shoulders sagged. "You ever wonder how life gets so screwed up?"

"I have."

"When Olivia first came by, my wife wouldn't have anything to do with her. I didn't think about Olivia much before that. After I talked to her that first time, though, all I kept thinking about was the years I missed. Same with JT. But then he showed up for the funeral and this crap situation with my legs, it made him stay."

Hailey slid her hand onto his knee. "It's time to get better now."

He sat quietly for a few seconds.

"Time out's over," Jack said abruptly as he reached down to check the brakes on his chair.

When he started his next set of reps, his effort was more sincere. By the end of the session, he was sweaty and his legs were trembling. She helped him cool down and couldn't keep the smile off her face. He was on his way now. Taking the steps he needed to get back on his feet.

After she congratulated Jack, she slipped away from the house as quietly as she could, hoping she wouldn't see JT.

She went home but couldn't settle down. She needed to do something to settle her mind, so she pulled out all of her mother's good silver and spread it out on the counter. When Sarah stopped by, Hailey sat her at the table with a cloth and a bottle of silver polish.

The sink was full of hot, sudsy water and the metallic scent of polish filled the air.

"Aren't you ever tempted to sell this all on eBay?" Sarah asked. Her friend was using a toothbrush to halfheartedly scrub the raised floral design on the edges of the heavy silver tea tray.

"If I did that, how would I release my stress?" Hailey said.

"Drugs."

"Polishing silver is the wiser choice."

"Not the funner choice, though, is it?"

"Funner, Sarah?"

"The fumes pickled my brain." She grabbed a cloth and started to rub the center of the tray. "What are you stressed about, anyway?"

"JT thinks I should set up a meeting with Olivia and Trevor. He had some good reasons."

Sarah dropped the cloth. Hailey concentrated on the tines of the fork she was rinsing.

"What do you think about that?"

One of the reasons Hailey loved Sarah was her friend's ability to take just about anybody and anything at face value. It wasn't that Sarah didn't have opinions, but she made sure she asked a few questions before she formed them.

"It's a terrible idea," Hailey said. "I've always thought it was a terrible idea."

"So why are you stressing about it now?"

Because she was doubting her decision. Trevor

had called the shots and she'd agreed to protect her daughter. But what if she'd been wrong? What if Olivia was better off with the truth, no matter how hard, than a shifting pile of questions?

And there was JT. Because she thought it was possible she was falling in love with her old boyfriend for the first time, and she knew nothing could come of it with this between them. But it was more than that.

"Maybe the way things have been with Jack is making me wonder about Trevor. If he had another chance would he come around the way Jack did? Olivia won't stop asking, and every time I put her off, I feel the space between us growing. What if someday she walks away completely?" Hailey said.

"Does JT have anything to do with the stress?"

JT had everything to do with it. A sudden panic rushed through her body. Hailey dropped the fork in the sink and tossed her rag in after it. She bent down, resting her forehead on her crossed arms on the edge of the sink. The steam from the water rose and heated her face.

"He scares me, Sarah."

Sarah was up and across the kitchen, her arms around Hailey's shoulders in less time than it took Hailey to draw in a deep breath and tamp down the sob she felt gathering at the back of her throat.

"What did he do?"

"He asked me to tell him the truth. To tell Olivia the truth."

"Oh, Hailey," Sarah said.

"But they don't understand. The truth is horrible. Why isn't it better to think I had a sweet, funny high-school boyfriend and we were stupid about birth control and too young to get married? Why isn't that the story they want?"

"Because it's not true," Sarah whispered.

"But the truth sucks. If I tell them the truth, won't they hate me?"

Sarah squeezed her shoulders but didn't say anything. She didn't need to. Hailey knew the answer to her question. JT was going to leave if she couldn't face up to this. And Olivia, Olivia would leave, too. Maybe not as soon as JT, but she was already starting to hate her mother.

"Remember when we became blood sisters?" Sarah asked. "Alice Harrison and Carmen Sarecen told everyone at recess that they did it, and we decided we would. We were up in your bedroom and we had that knife, the little steak knife? And later we found out Alice and Carmen used a pin. But you sliced your thumb with the knife and there was all that blood?"

Sarah paused. Hailey nodded. She still had her head down. She could recall the scene clearly. She'd been horrified by the blood and her thumb had really hurt.

"You dropped the knife and I picked it up and I held out my finger and the last thing I wanted to do was cut myself. But you were absolutely dripping blood and all you kept saying was your mother was going to kill you for getting blood on the quilt."

Hailey didn't think they'd ever talked about this. She rubbed her index finger against the pad of her thumb where the thin line of the scar remained.

"So I sliced my thumb. It didn't hurt at first but then it started to throb and I was bleeding, too, and then you reached for my hand and we held our thumbs together. And then we were blood sisters and everything was okay."

"It was not okay. I got grounded."

"And Alice and Carmen made fun of us for weeks."

Hailey almost laughed, but she was afraid if she did she'd really cry. She was tired of crying. "What exactly was the point of that story?"

"I sliced my finger open because you were waiting for me. Sometimes if you want something bad enough, you have to make the first move. If the other person wants to be with you bad enough, they'll catch up."

"But how can I let them know the truth? It's not me. Not the person I want to be. I slept with my teacher because he was hot and I was tired of being good and he made me feel grown-up. Why would they want to know I was drunk the first time we had sex and drunk the second time, and I never even liked him very much but I was so caught up in the excitement that I didn't realize that until it was too late?"

"Hailey, they don't want to know that. But the point is, that's you. We all have things about ourselves we hate. But if you keep it all covered up, well, there's not a whole lot left for people who want to love you to work with."

"I'm scared."

"If you decide to do it, you won't be alone. Remember, you'll be one step ahead, but I guarantee they'll be ready to catch up. You just have to give them the chance."

SHE DROVE TO Trevor's street and parked. She used to do this sometimes right after Olivia was born. She'd leave the baby with her parents and drive here and stop far enough away that he couldn't see her car from his windows. Then she'd stare. She'd memorized the outside of his house and his and Julia's cars and even the metallic-blue raincoat Julia had worn that wet spring. Hailey would watch and memorize and imagine herself and Olivia and what place they might have in those scenes.

She hadn't been back in years. Her goal now was completely different. She wasn't searching for a place for them, but trying to see through the facade into the man. If she offered him a chance to get to know his daughter, would he do the right thing? Hailey knew he'd never love Olivia the way she did. How could he? But if he'd only unbend enough to admit she was his. To talk to her, invite her to dinner a few times a year. That wasn't much, but it could be enough.

As she watched, a car pulled into the driveway and Trevor and Julia stepped out. They walked toward the house, laughing, his hand on her elbow.

She felt a quick bite of anger. Trevor had what he wanted. Everything he wanted. He'd kept his job, his wife and his lifestyle. Sarah had told Hailey about a few other affairs he'd had over the years. His threat toward her child had kept her silent, but now, Hailey thought, she and Olivia were going to get what *they* wanted.

She called Information, got his number and waited while it rang. When she heard his voice, she shut her eyes, too nervous to do this when she was so close to his house and to him.

"Trevor?" she said. Then she cleared her throat. She wasn't the teenage girl she'd been the last time she'd tried this. She was a woman now, with a daughter who needed her to stand up and be strong and get her this part of the life she wanted. "It's Hailey Maddox."

She heard a click as he hung up on her. She opened her eyes and dialed again.

"I'm outside in my car. Would you prefer if I came to the door?" she said without preamble.

"Just a moment," he said.

She heard rustling and a door close on his end.

"What is it?"

"I'd like to ask you to meet with Olivia. I'd like to let her know who her father is."

"Surely after all this time there is no need to—"

"You're her father. There's a need."

He didn't respond, so she pushed on. "She's looking for her father. It's entirely possible she's going to find you on her own. I think it's best if we manage this before that happens."

"I'm not entirely…but if she's trying to… I see your point. I see how this needs to be managed."

Hailey seized on this apparent concession.

"You can set the rules. Just tell me what you want so I can prepare her."

"I can set the rules?" he asked.

"Yes. Within reason, of course."

"Of course."

There was a pause and then he said, "Fine. Maybe it is time."

He told her that Julia would be out of town the next weekend and Hailey could bring Olivia by then.

Hailey sat with the phone open in her hand. She hadn't expected that. He'd sounded reasonable, telling her to bring Olivia at lunchtime on Sunday so they could have a meal to help avoid any awkwardness. Was it possible this was going to work out? If Trevor acknowledged Olivia, how much of the bad feelings would that clear away? Could Hailey hope there was a chance for her, too? For her and JT?

JT HADN'T SEEN HAILEY in days. Jack had set up a new schedule and was going to Viva every other day. But JT dropped him off outside and didn't go in. If she'd wanted to see him, she knew exactly where he was. Obviously she wasn't interested.

He'd called Terrance and set up a plan to go into

the office for the day on Friday. Olivia had agreed to stay with his dad and Charlie was going to cover the night. JT was flying back on Saturday. But he knew, he thought they all knew, this was the beginning of the end.

He was nervous about talking to Terrance. He knew it was more than likely the end of RoboGen, as well. But if the past few days had taught him anything it was that he was absolutely not cut out for taking risks. He didn't want to live this way all the time, no matter what the reward on the other end was.

Ironically he'd done a decent draft design. He stared at his screen, where the telescope mount for the NASA project seemed to mock him as it revolved slowly in just about finished 3D. He was finished with a solid pass on the mount and he hadn't even told Terrance he was starting it.

He stared at the mount. It looked good, and more than that, he knew it met the technical challenges NASA had laid out in the spec, including the criteria for sand resistance in the unforgiving Martian landscape, which had given him fits.

But that only meant he had even less interest in submitting the design. If he didn't care or didn't think he had a chance, he could tell Terrance to go ahead. Putting something he cared about out there was a different story. This bid was only the first one—Terrance wanted their whole business to shift to the kind of work JT wouldn't be able to help getting invested in.

CHAPTER TWELVE

WHEN JT PULLED INTO the parking lot at RoboGen, Terrance's car was already there. He dragged his card key out of his pocket and let himself in. He'd been so proud the day they opened this office. It was as if they'd hit the big time when they got their own building.

Their assistant, Jeannie, jumped up when she saw him and ran to give him a huge hug. She was short and stocky, and had been on a rowing team as long as he'd known her. A hug from Jeannie wasn't something you could ignore. He put his arms around her and hugged back.

"I'm so sorry about your mother," she said.

He patted her, not wanting her to hear that he was choked up. Jeannie was in her early fifties and had been with RoboGen since before it was RoboGen. Back when it was just him and Terrance and their old partner, Glenn, with one undergraduate intern trying to figure out how to make things work.

A big part of why things did work was because they'd listened to Jeannie. She was one of the people in JT's life he counted on to keep him grounded, and he'd missed her more than he realized. It was good to be back. He just hoped he'd be able to stay.

"Terrance in?" he asked.

Jeannie pointed to the closed door of the conference room. "He's in there. I think you have him scared," she said. "I keep telling him you have to listen to each other but he's scared."

"The man should know enough to listen to you."

"You're the one he's been missing."

JT lifted his backpack and smiled. "No time like the present."

"You want coffee?" she asked.

"If you want to be in on this meeting, you can just ask. You don't have to pretend you're the kind of assistant who brings me coffee."

She waved him toward the conference room. "You go ahead. We'll talk later."

Terrance didn't turn around from his computer screen when JT pushed the conference-room door open. "I'm in here," he said.

"Good. Because you're the one I'm trying to find."

Terrance pushed back from the table slowly. "You are a sight for sore eyes," he said.

JT let Terrance hug him and he hugged back, feeling like a traitor the entire time.

JT sat in one of the empty chairs, setting his backpack on the chair next to him. He knew Terrance would be champing at the bit to start their meeting.

But to his surprise, his partner stopped him with a hand on his arm. "Wait, hang on, JT. How's your dad? How are you?"

The last thing he wanted was to drag any of that out right now. He needed to focus on Terrance and get him to understand why they needed to pull back from expansion. RoboGen was his home now and he was going to make sure it stayed manageable. Stayed safe.

"He's getting better. Said he might be able to get up on crutches next week. Be a nice change from the wheelchair."

Terrance smiled. "That's progress, man. Really great."

"Yeah."

Neither of them spoke for a beat and then Terrance went on. "See, Jeannie told me to stop pushing you. Said you'd never responded well to that and if I stopped bringing the NASA project up and stopped saying expansion, you'd come around in your own time on your own terms. So I'm not asking about it. Isn't Jeannie smart?"

"She'd kick my ass at *Jeopardy*." Which he happened to know for a fact. She was the reigning champion at their annual company board game challenge day.

Another beat of silence.

"So I'm still not asking," Terrance said hopefully.

"Okay." JT felt impatient with them both. "Can you tell me again why you want this?"

"Seriously?"

"No." JT stood and walked to the window. "Not really. I… What if it doesn't work? What if we throw everything we have into this and we don't get the bid? Or we get one bid and we never get another?"

"We'll get it."

"No. I don't mean reassure me that we'll get it. What do we do if we don't?"

"Nothing. We recover from the crushing blow to our egos and we move on. Unless Jordan Robotics gets it. If they do, then we recover from the crushing blow to our egos, torch the Jordan Robotics headquarters, preferably with that prick Glenn Jordan inside, and then we move on."

JT snorted. "I hate that guy."

"Whatever. He doesn't matter. What matters is why you're asking."

"It feels wrong to abandon what we have. This business is working. How many small businesses can say that? We pay our people on time. They have health care. We have a solid base here. Why would we mess with it?"

"But JT, our stuff can be in space. Mars, baby. That's why we're doing this." Terrance's voice held all the longing and excitement JT felt every time he thought about that.

Way back when he'd started working at his dad's garage and realized there were problems you could fix with just your brain and some tools—no drama, no fights; just apply what you know and do your work carefully—he'd fallen in love with the mechanical world. And then when he'd grown older and realized that those same things—brains and tools put together—could take you places you'd never been, well, he'd known what he wanted to do.

JT let Terrance's words sink in. Wasn't like he didn't know that was the reason for them both. Terrance loved the corporate stuff; building an empire had been his career plan probably since preschool. But they were partners because they shared that same dream: making inventions that would be in space. So what if Terrance's dream included org charts and JT's fitted parts together? They were partners and they'd always known where they were headed.

"I know. But I can't," he said quietly.

"Don't do this, JT."

"Don't do what?"

"Don't do what you do. Don't back off because you're close."

"I'm not. I… What are you even talking about?"

"I'm talking about you and your pathological aversion to risk."

"Don't give me that psychoanalytical crap. I have legitimate business questions about this. How can we handle the extra capacity? What if we're taking on too much and it puts us out of business? We have twelve people and their families depending on us now and we're talking about adding forty more."

"And it scares you white that your design might

win and we'll have to go to the next level and you'll have to do this all over again with even more at stake," Terrance said with firm conviction. JT didn't like the uncomfortable feeling that he was so transparent.

"I'm not afraid of losing."

"I know," Terrance said. "You're afraid to try. You're afraid to admit that you want this as much as I do. Face it, JT. You just have this idea that you're not supposed to try."

JT's frustration boiled up. He was sick of people telling him he didn't try hard enough. Sometimes trying was just idiocy. Sometimes trying got you nowhere or left you someplace worse than where you'd been when you started.

"I drew up a design. It's preliminary. You'll need to have the team look at it and set up a testing plan. I made notes on that." He picked up his backpack. "I'll put the files on the server this morning. I'm cleaning out my desk and I'll be gone in a couple hours."

Terrance sat in shock long enough to let JT get almost out the door. But then he shot out of his chair and flung himself in front of JT.

"What the hell are you talking about?"

"I thought about it. I love the designing. I love the idea of space. But if we make the company bigger, everything is going to ride on my designs. We'll hire more people and they'll all depend on me. Jeannie has three more years of college for Robert. What if the company goes under before he graduates? And you sat with me at Emily and

Parker's wedding last year. She's due at Christmas and the two of them plus that baby, they'll depend on me. I don't want it. I don't want any part of it."

"But you don't have to quit."

JT almost growled, he was so frustrated. "You can't talk me into this, Terrance. I don't *want* it."

"Fine. We won't expand. Nobody ever said we were doing it without you."

JT stared at him.

"I'm not freaking Glenn Jordan here, buddy. This ride has always been ours from the start. If RoboGen stays the way it's been, well, I won't say I'm not disappointed. And I can't promise I won't ever bring this up again. But I don't… I never said I wanted you to leave."

"You'd be okay with things the way they are?"

"Define okay," Terrance said. But he was smiling. "I'll deal with it."

"What about everything you've been saying? We've been going around on this since January."

"I took a shot, JT. Gave it everything I had. That's how I am."

JT nodded. But he also knew, and had just seen it proved once again, that Terrance was one of the most stand-up guys ever. He couldn't believe Terrance wanted him to stay more than he wanted to expand. That was going to take some time to sink in. But he was relieved.

"I appreciate this," JT said.

"Jeannie would have my head if I let you quit."

He went to his office and shut the door. The

place smelled stale, but he needed some privacy. He opened his laptop and pulled up the sketch for the NASA telescope mount. It was weird. Looking at it now, knowing he didn't have to chase that particular long shot anymore, he felt empty.

Which was crazy. He'd gotten everything he wanted. His life was safe. No one expected him to do more than he was ready to do. He should be happy.

It might take a few weeks, but he'd be back here soon, working on the same projects, eating takeout or grilling on his porch, playing Frisbee whenever he could. Just how he wanted it.

He leaned back and stared at the star chart he had mounted on the wall opposite his desk. He should take that down, he thought. Having it there was as fake as anything Hailey ever did. He'd been saying all these years that what he wanted was a shot at space, but now he'd just turned that down. Time to get used to his life the way it really was.

He wondered if his dad was at Viva. Had Olivia gone with him? And most of all, JT wondered where Hailey was. Did she know he'd left town? Did she care?

He shut his laptop and closed his eyes. There had to be a way he could do this. Be here. Because this was his life and he needed to accept that. He'd gotten just what he wanted. No risks. No fear of failure. Just this.

HAILEY HAD ASKED SARAH to build a fire for her in the patio fireplace. She herself had stacked a small pile of logs nearby and pulled two chairs up close. On the table between the chairs she'd set out a bowl of M&M's—a gift from Sarah—two glasses of water with lemon and Olivia's baby book.

Now all she was waiting for was her daughter.

She stood up nervously and waved Olivia over as soon as she spotted her coming down the driveway. Olivia rolled her eyes but crossed the gravel and came up onto the patio. "What's this, Mom? I have to get home. Molly's supposed to call."

"We have things to discuss, Olivia. Please." She gestured to the other chair. Olivia sat down and then really looked at Hailey for the first time.

"What are you wearing?"

Hailey had gone out that afternoon to the mall and searched until she found the shirt she had on. She knew there were no rules about how to dress for the conversation in which you tell your daughter who her father really is, but she'd hoped Olivia would appreciate the gesture. Her shirt was black and said "I Want to Believe." She knew it was a quote from *The X-Files* and if she hadn't, the green alien printed underneath would have been a clue. But it also summed up what she hoped she could tell Olivia about her dad.

"It's my new shirt."

"That's *yours?*"

When Hailey nodded, Olivia sat back in her chair. Apparently now she was convinced her mother was serious about having a conversation.

"I lied to you. I don't think we need to go back over all the reasons why that was a bad idea, but I did it because I love you." She picked up the baby book, the first scrapbook she'd ever made. "When we're finished here, if you would just read this. Look at the pictures. And think about how I felt. I was eighteen when you were born, Olivia. I was scared and alone, and a lot of people had turned their backs on me because they were angry. Your grandparents were already so upset and I just needed someone to be on my side. JT was there."

Hailey clenched her jaw and swallowed. She didn't want to cry.

"I didn't love JT. But he, well, he was one in a million. I wish I'd known. Anyway, there were problems between me and your real dad, and I wanted you to have someone. I didn't think it would hurt anyone if I gave you JT. I didn't realize all the ways that would get twisted. I just wanted you to be happy."

Olivia crossed her arms on her chest. "It was wrong, Mom."

"I'm so sorry," Hailey said.

Olivia's expression didn't change.

"You convinced me I had done the wrong thing. So I got in touch with your father. He agreed to meet with you this weekend." Hailey put her hand on Olivia's knee. "It's hard, honey, because you know him. So I'll just say it. Trevor Meyers is your dad."

Olivia's mouth worked before she managed to speak. "Mr. Meyers? From school?"

Hailey nodded.

"But he… I knew him."

Olivia started to cry. Tears welled up and she tried to wipe them away but they came too fast. Hailey slid off her chair onto the patio and crouched next to her daughter, trying to find a way that she could wrap Olivia up as she'd done when the girl was tiny.

"I'm so sorry," she repeated over and over. "I'm so sorry."

"Did he know?" Olivia choked out. "All this time, did he know?"

"He did," Hailey said. "But he wants to see you, sweetie. He said it was okay."

"But he never…" Olivia sniffed. "He never wanted to be with me before this. Why hasn't he ever been here?"

"I don't know," Hailey said. "He was mad at me. Worried about his marriage, his job. I was his student—he'd have been fired. You don't have to meet him."

"Why didn't you tell me then?"

"He convinced me not to."

"Like a threat?"

Hailey nodded.

Olivia stood up. "No. I want to. I want to do it." She was still crying. "I can't be with you right now."

Hailey nodded. "Molly's? Keep your phone on?"

"All right." Olivia grabbed the baby book before she left, and Hailey tried to convince herself that this was going to be the right thing for them all. Somehow.

JT HAD FLOWN BACK on Saturday and found Jack in an uproar. "It's a lucky goddamn thing you showed up today!" he yelled. "Olivia's meeting her dad."

"What?"

"Hailey finally came clean and she's set up a meeting. Trevor Meyers, that prick. He must be almost ten years older than Hailey."

JT dropped into a chair at the table. "Trevor Meyers? He was her art teacher."

He felt sick just thinking about it. Meyers hadn't stopped at an affair with a married woman—he'd slept with Hailey, too, and then he'd abandoned her when she was pregnant. JT could feel the blood pounding in his head.

"That's why I'm not letting Olivia go in there alone. That guy is a jerk and you don't know what he's going to pull."

"We're going?" JT asked.

"Damn right we're going," Jack replied. He was dressed in jeans and a khaki work shirt with the sleeves rolled up. Even in his wheelchair he didn't look like a guy you'd want to mess with. "Call your brother."

"Charlie?" JT wasn't sure that was a good idea. "He's not much for the public spectacle."

In fact, if there was anything Charlie hated more than witnessing a public spectacle, it was being part of a public spectacle.

"Nobody's making a spectacle of anybody," Jack

said. "Unless Meyers starts it. Then there will be a spectacle and your brother should be there to help."

"Help what?"

"Help you hold me back."

JT pulled out his phone. "Right. Because that's what I'm going to be doing. Worrying about holding you back."

They made Charlie drive them, figuring he had the nicest car and that might help them convince any possible police officers that they were upstanding citizens. They didn't mention that reasoning to Charlie, though. JT told him he had to drive because he was the youngest.

Charlie stopped for the light on Oak and his eyes met JT's in the rearview mirror. "I always hated Trevor Meyers," he said. "If it wouldn't screw Olivia up, I'd be hoping he'd make a wrong move."

Jack pointed at JT. "I told you he'd want to be here."

JT settled back in the seat. He was glad they were doing this, but like Charlie, he was hoping it would be entirely unnecessary. Not that he wouldn't love to unload all of his anger directly onto Trevor's face, but that was selfish. He wanted this to work out. He wanted Trevor to find that decent core inside himself that would enable him to do the right thing. If it didn't work out, if Olivia ended up hurt because he'd pushed Hailey into taking this chance, JT would never forgive himself. And he was sure Hailey would never forgive him, either.

Charlie eased into a parking spot behind a minivan about three houses down from Trevor's. There was no sign of the Mustang yet, so Hailey and Olivia probably hadn't arrived. The three McNultys scrunched down in their seats and tried to appear both innocent and invisible at the same time.

JT wished Hailey had told him. He was glad Olivia was getting the chance to know her dad. But he wished Hailey could have trusted him. He thought back, trying to pinpoint times when he should have seen what was happening, but there was nothing. He'd been so convinced that Hailey was exactly who she seemed, he'd never looked any deeper.

He'd said he loved her, but she was right. He had loved the idea of her. Now, though, knowing how hard this was for her, but that she was doing it for her kid? Having seen her struggle with his dad, pulling him along to the point where he was ready to help himself. All the ways she made her clients feel at home and safe so they could focus on getting well. Hailey wasn't perfect. But she was fantastic. He wished he'd had the chance to tell her that.

OLIVIA SAT STIFFLY in the passenger seat as they drove to Trevor's house. "Do you think he's going to, like, when we're in school, say hi. Or whatever?"

"I don't know what he'll want. Remember I told him we would follow his lead."

"I know. I mean, I hardly ever see him at school—he's mostly in his office. But if I did. I wonder..." Olivia trailed off and skipped to a new thought. "What about Molly? Do you think he'll care if the other kids know? I mean, if it's not a secret anymore with us, it won't be a secret at all, right?"

Hailey didn't like the way Olivia's thoughts were rushing. "We have to wait and see, sweetie. We don't know what he's going to want."

"Right. Right." Olivia sounded as if she was trying to calm herself down. But then she smiled. "It doesn't matter, though. None of it matters. I just want to talk to him."

"Well, that certainly seems like the plan for today," Hailey said.

She parked in front of the house and led the way up the stairs, Olivia suddenly shy, walking a few steps behind her. The doorbell echoed inside the big house and then Trevor was there, holding the door open and motioning them in.

JT WATCHED HAILEY and Olivia walk up the steps and ring the doorbell. By the time the door opened and they walked in, he'd squeezed his fists so tight he couldn't feel his fingers.

"Olivia looked nervous," he said. "She only hunches her shoulders like that when she's nervous."

"Meyers is the one who should be nervous," Jack replied. "Guy better know what's good for him." He banged his hand on the seat. "I can't believe I'm crippled. Get my chair out in case we need to go in."

JT got his chair out onto the sidewalk and helped his dad into it. Then they settled back to wait, him and Charlie leaning on the car, Jack hunched in his chair, all three of them watching the front door intently.

SHE'D SEEN HIM so many times over the years. She'd trained herself not to react to his presence. But being in his house, with Olivia, on his turf… With him holding the cards, she felt nauseous.

He was handsome in a bland, frat-boy way, his brown hair still thick and his green eyes standing out against dark lashes.

"I wasn't sure you'd come," he said to her. "Hello, Olivia."

Hailey expected that he'd take them into the living room or straight to the dining room to eat, but he didn't. He stood between them and the rest of the house, keeping them crowded close to the shut door behind them.

"Hello, Mr. Meyers," Olivia said quietly.

He didn't seem to hear her.

"Well, I hope this won't take long. As I said, Julia is away for the weekend, but I have a tee time." He glanced at his watch. "Only forty minutes before I need to be on the course."

Hailey knew right then this was wrong. She recognized the coldness in his voice from the last time they'd discussed Olivia. He hadn't changed. He'd let them come here to teach her a lesson, to show her, again, that he was in control so she wouldn't threaten his marriage or his job or his standing. He'd always liked to play power games with her, and while this wasn't a game, it was definitely about his need to dominate.

She grabbed Olivia's hand, pulling her daughter close and fumbling for the door behind her. He reached over her and held the door shut firmly with one hand.

"Don't leave now, Hailey. I don't want to have to do this again. I thought you'd have understood me by now, but maybe the third time's the charm."

Olivia was staring at her father as Hailey tugged on the door handle. He was stronger than her, though, and she couldn't make it budge.

"Stop it, Trevor. Let us go and we won't come back."

"Mom," cried Olivia. "Not yet."

"Yes, *Mom,* don't go yet."

Hailey gave up on the door handle. She turned back to scan the room, looking for another exit.

"Olivia, I explained this to your mother twice already, but she seems unable to understand."

"Please don't, Trevor. Don't do this to her."

"We agreed to do this according to my rules and I told you my rules a long time ago. You're the one who forced this. Rule number one..." His voice rose, but not ever to an extreme. There was nothing to show that he was tearing her daughter's heart out right in front of her. "I may be the man whose sperm created you, but I won't have anything to do with you. Ever."

Olivia gasped and shrank against Hailey.

"Rule number two. You can take me to court and prove I'm your biological father. That will have no impact on rule number one. I will have nothing to do with you. Ever."

Hailey tightened her grip on Olivia's hand and then, just as Trevor was gathering breath for his next pronouncement, she cocked her fist and gave him a hard, close-range punch to the neck. Physical therapists were well-trained in the vulnerabilities of the human body.

When he doubled over, choking, she kneed him in the groin. She was breathing hard as he crumpled to the floor at their feet. "Don't speak to my daughter again."

She wrenched the door open and pulled Olivia outside, then stumbled down the steps, blind with angry tears. They were almost to the car when the McNultys charged up, JT and Charlie in the lead, Jack pushing his chair furiously, a few paces behind.

"Are you okay?" JT asked. "Did he hurt you?"

Charlie was a few feet behind JT, clearly ready to rush Trevor's front door.

What were they doing here? Why would JT be here? Had he thought everything would work out fine after she did what he demanded, and then he could just step in and have part of her life, too?

"He didn't hurt us," she snapped. "Not that way. He…said things…." She gestured to Olivia, who was trying to stop crying, taking gulping breaths that shuddered through her body. Hailey was so angry she was shaking. What a stupid, stupid fool she'd been. "We never should have done this. I knew this was a bad idea. I knew nothing good would come of it. I wish I'd never listened to you, because this did nothing. Nothing!"

The color drained out of JT's face at her attack but Olivia whirled on her, "Don't yell at him. Don't you dare. I wanted this!" she shouted. "I'm the one. And it was good. Now I'm not wondering about my dad, thinking there's someone somewhere who wants me." She choked on a sob.

Jack reached them just as she stopped. He braked his chair and opened his arms. Olivia buried her face in his shirt and held on. Jack wrapped his arms around her, and he made the tall, teenage girl look tiny. Hailey was crying now, too.

"I'm sorry," JT said quietly. "I never meant… I wouldn't have hurt her for anything. You know that."

JT was furious with Meyers. But that wasn't the point. Right here, right now, he had something he needed to do. He was pretty sure it was too little too late, and he wished he'd done it before, but he was doing it now. He wasn't going to step away until he'd seen it through.

"Olivia's right, Hailey. She wanted to know who her dad was and now she knows." JT had a few thoughts about Meyers, but he wouldn't say them in front of the girl. She'd straightened up, and while she was still clutching his dad's hand, she was listening. "And the other thing she wanted to know was if there was someone out there who loved her. And she's got that, too." He pointed at Charlie and Jack and himself. "This thing between us started out as a lie, but it's not a lie anymore. I don't know what the hell you'd call it, but there's probably some word for a family you get when you take a fake grandpa and a granddaughter who won't give up and a whole bunch of other stubborn people and put them together. So that's what we have. What I'm offering. If you want it."

Charlie stepped forward and Jack gave him a thumbs-up. Hailey looked from one to the other of them and realized he was right. These people knew her. They knew everything she'd done and they'd seen all the harm that had caused. And still on the day when she needed backup, they'd been there. She hadn't even needed to ask. They came here for her and Olivia and stood by them.

She took a step forward on the sidewalk and JT took one, and they were together and his arms were around her. She grabbed hold of him, pressing her face into his "Huck It Deep" T-shirt and knowing this was her home. No matter what. She was home.

"SWEETIE, I'M SORRY." Hailey said. "I should have known he'd do something like that. He's just so controlling."

She and Olivia were in the kitchen at their house. Olivia had begged to be taken home, and then spent quite a long time in the shower. When she came out, she was dressed in a ratty yellow T-shirt from her Statlerville High gym uniform and had pulled her hair back in a ponytail. Her clothes from the morning were all in a plastic bag and she asked Hailey if it was okay to throw them away.

When she closed the back door, she sat across from Hailey.

"Is that why you wouldn't tell me? You were protecting me."

Hailey nodded.

Olivia surprised her by grabbing her hand. "I'm sorry I kept pushing. I didn't make this easy for you."

Hailey shook her hand gently from side to side. "Kids aren't supposed to make things easy on their parents."

"But I'm glad it happened this way. That we went together. I'm glad I didn't figure it out without you. Now when I think about him, I can picture that punch."

Hailey smiled. Her knuckles were throbbing, but she welcomed the pain. Trevor's throat and—other parts—were probably in much worse shape.

"I never knew you could fight like that." Hailey hadn't actually known she could, either—theory was one thing, actually hitting him was something else—but she gave her daughter a mysterious glance and said, "There are many things you don't know about me."

"I…" Olivia hesitated. "I don't want to tell anyone about him."

"Okay, but this time it's on your terms, not his."

Olivia's hands twisted in her lap. "Would he lose his job if we told the school about you?"

"Probably. I was eighteen so it wasn't a crime, but he was a teacher."

"Then I think we should tell. So he can't take advantage of another girl."

"People will find out then."

"I'll be okay," Olivia said, her eyes on Hailey. She felt the trust behind that simple nod, the reassurance that there wasn't anything between them that they couldn't address, and she knew that whatever else had happened at Trevor's, she'd gotten her daughter back.

She'd been so afraid that Olivia wouldn't be able to handle this, that she'd be permanently damaged by it, but seeing her now, Hailey knew that Olivia would be okay. Trevor would never be in her life, but they didn't need him to be complete.

Then Olivia said, "Maybe I could just keep pretending it's JT. I like him."

"We can't do that anymore. He's been through enough for our sakes." Hailey was proud to see Olivia nod. They would figure out how to stand on their own together. "But he likes *you,* Olivia. You can still be friends with him, even without that."

A small but most welcome smirk appeared on Olivia's face. "Are you going to be friends with him, too, Mom?"

Hailey stood and reached for her daughter's hand. "I'm going to try."

"Now?"

"Right now."

THE LATE-AFTERNOON SUN played up the polish on the black granite countertops in the kitchen. JT looked across the table at his dad. They'd gotten back from Meyers's house ten minutes ago.

After Hailey and Olivia left, they'd gone up to Meyers's house and had explained to him, in what JT thought were convincing terms, that in the future he should stay far away from anyone the McNultys cared about. Meyers, looking pale and shaky, hadn't seemed in any condition to argue, but Jack had punched him once just to make sure he understood.

"You leaving again?" Jack said finally.

"Not today."

"What about work? You and Terrance figure things out?"

"I guess." The relief he'd expected still hadn't materialized.

JT stood and grabbed a glass, filling it with water. He really didn't need an interrogation from his dad.

"I asked your mom for the divorce because of Olivia. That's funny, isn't it? Her real dad doesn't want anything to do with her, and I broke up my marriage because your mom wouldn't let her be in our lives."

JT stared. "That's why?"

"Not only that. Olivia made me think about a lot of stuff. You. Us. How we ended up the way we did."

"I'm sorry I left," JT said.

"I think your mom was jealous," Jack stated. He rubbed his hand in a circle on the smooth wooden tabletop. "When she made you pick us or Hailey, you picked wrong in her eyes."

JT shook his head. "I wasn't picking her. It was just that she needed me."

Jack looked at him thoughtfully. "I know. And that's what made me so mad."

"Which part?"

"The part where I was afraid you were going to end up like me. Stuck with Hailey before you got a chance to think about what that meant. I loved your mom, JT, but she made my life a living hell a lot of the time. I didn't want that for you."

"Hailey's not like Mom."

"I know that now." Jack rubbed his face. "I misjudged you, too. I never thought you'd really stay gone."

"Because you didn't think I could make it on my own." JT said it with no emotion, even though it hurt to say.

"No. No. I never thought that." Jack struggled to get his words out. "I…I never knew you to hold a grudge. Your whole life, you always came back for more."

"It wasn't a grudge," JT said, all the old hurt washing over him. "I came to you for help, begged you to help me help her, and you told me to get out and not come back."

"Fair enough." Jack sighed. "I called you a whole bunch of times. Well, almost called you. Dialed all the numbers but one and then hung up. Wish I'd dialed the whole thing."

JT nodded his head repeatedly, as if he was mulling over a decision, letting it sink in. He was really trying to listen to his dad, but it was hard. "I'd have answered. If you'd called."

Jack's face twisted and JT realized he'd hurt him. And he didn't want this conversation to go that way. They were really talking, and maybe with this behind them, there'd be something new to build on. So JT threw his dad a line.

"But you asked me to stay. That means something."

"Been good," Jack responded quickly.

"Sorry I'm such a moron," JT said, trying to lighten the mood, but Jack surprised him by tapping the table.

"Come over here, son."

JT walked toward him, and when he was close, Jack reached out and wrapped one big work-hardened hand around his neck and pulled him even close. For the first time JT could remember, his dad kissed him on top of his head and whispered gruffly, "If you really were a moron I wouldn't call you one. You know that."

Truthfully, JT wasn't sure he did. Jack had called him and everyone else plenty of names both deserved and undeserved, and probably that wasn't going to change. But he did figure his dad meant to tell him something good just then. Something about approval and acceptance and love.

"Thanks, Dad," he said. And he meant a lot more than thanks for the lie, but he figured even if Jack never understood exactly what he meant, they wouldn't lose track of each other again. The strength of that one lie and one thank-you would keep them together while they built a new relationship. Which was a good thing, all right. A really good thing.

JT stepped back and nodded. "You know what, Dad? I'm finished messing around." He threw his cell phone on the table. "If Hailey calls, answer it."

"Where are you going to be?"

"I have to call Terrance. We have plans to make."

"I thought you already talked things out with him."

"I made a mistake." JT caught his dad's eye. "Good thing it's not too late to change."

THE DOORBELL RANG while he and Jack were in the family room watching the Phillies lose to the Pirates. JT heard Olivia first, her voice calling through the screen door.

"Send her in here. We'll stay out of your way," Jack said as JT got up. His dad stopped him. "Try not to mess this up. I like that girl and her mom."

"Yes, sir," he said. "I'll do my best."

When he got to the living room, Olivia and Hailey were still standing on the porch. "Come in," he called.

Olivia's face was blotchy and he guessed she'd been crying. He wasn't sure what to say, but she knew exactly what she wanted. She walked straight to him and wrapped her arms around his waist. "My dad is worse than a schmuck," she whispered. "Thanks for being a much better fake dad and for teaching me how to play Frisbee and for not being a horrible jerk."

Before he had a chance to do much more than pat her back, she'd unwrapped herself and walked through into the family room.

He looked up at Hailey, who stood just inside the door. "That was a little inarticulate, but she meant it."

"It's okay. The hug said it all anyway. You want to sit outside for a minute?".

She nodded.

They went out to the back porch and settled on the top step.

"You're sure he didn't hit you?" he asked.

"I hit him." She held out her hand to show him her bruised knuckles. "He blocked the door. I should never have met him at his house. Neutral territory would have been better. Maybe it wouldn't have gotten out of hand." She paused. "No. I can't control him, can I? No matter how carefully I planned this, it would have gone wrong."

He held her hand gently in his, brushing the pad of his thumb across her knuckles so softly it felt like a breath. She shivered.

"It wasn't all bad, though," JT said. "I mean, it hurts now. And Olivia's going to have a lot to deal with. But at least it's out in the open and you can handle it now."

"We can," she said softly.

"I talked to my dad. We're going to be fine. I called Terrance. He's been pushing me to do this big expansion and I said okay but only if I can have an office here."

His ears were still ringing from the whoop

Terrance had let out. JT knew they had a lot of work to do, but the thing was, he wasn't nervous. With everything he and Terrance had built, they would take care of their company and grow in smart ways, and someday, he was sure of it, he'd have something he'd made in space.

"But what—"

He brought his hands around and cupped Hailey's face. "We're all going to be fine. If it's what you want."

"Oh, JT, I know what you must think of me now that you know about Trevor. I'm sorry. I was young, naive, selfish. But I understand if you can't… It's okay. As long as Olivia is happy."

A tear started down her face, but he brushed it away. He moved his hands to her shoulders, his fingers offering a gentle pressure.

"What I think, Hailey? I think Trevor Meyers is a son of a bitch who took advantage of a student. I think you made bad choices but no worse than any of us. I think you're loyal and brave and the way you protected your daughter is an inspiration to me."

He bent his head, his voice softening. "I think I wish I'd gotten to know you back then instead of spending so much time imagining a perfect girlfriend. That was unfair—if perfection is the standard, none of us can compete. I'm sorry I put that on you. Sorry I made it hard for you to turn to me."

"I did turn to you, though. You were right there,

and you've always been right there. I didn't give you enough credit even though the evidence was staring me in the face."

He closed his eyes and then leaned down to kiss her, a long, lingering kiss full of longing and fulfillment and promise. It was everything she needed and then some. She tilted her head and moved closer to feel more of him, to press herself against him. Now that they were back together she didn't want to let him go.

He held his wrist up. "It's exactly three-thirteen, eastern standard time. We'll start the clock over."

"Thank goodness we know the accurate time."

"You want to go out with me, Hailey?"

"You bet, JT."

He brought her hand to his mouth and kissed her knuckles. "I never kissed a boxer before."

She slapped his arm, saying, "I'm dangerous, pal—don't you forget it," and then pulled him close to kiss again.

A loud banging from the family room startled her, and she pulled back her head.

"JT!" Jack yelled. "Olivia and I want some dinner. We have any eggs?"

"I'm going to kill him," JT muttered.

But he was grinning. They did have eggs. And Charlie was coming over later with pizza. JT had called in an order for the "Dessert for Twelve" tier thing again and Charlie had said he'd pick that up, too. There wasn't one thing JT needed to be doing right now. So he bent his head and kissed Hailey. He figured he could keep himself occupied that way for a good long time.

* * * * *

In honor of our 60th anniversary,
Harlequin® American Romance® is celebrating
by featuring an all-American male each month,
all year long with
MEN MADE IN AMERICA!
This June, we'll be featuring American men
living in the West.

Here's a sneak preview of
THE CHIEF RANGER by Rebecca Winters.

Chief Ranger Vance Rossiter has to confront the sister of a man who died while under Vance's watch...and also confront his attraction to her.

"Chief Ranger Rossiter?" The sight of the woman who'd stepped inside Vance's office brought him to his feet. "I'm Rachel Darrow. Your secretary said I should come right in."

"Please," he said, walking around his desk to shake her hand. At a glance he estimated she was in her midtwenties. Her feminine curves did wonders for the pale-blue T-shirt and jeans she was wearing. "Ranger Jarvis informed me there's a young boy with you."

The unfriendly expression in her beautiful green eyes caught him off guard. "Yes," was her clipped reply. "When we arrived in Yosemite the ranger told me I couldn't go anywhere in the park until I talked to you first."

"That's right."

"Knowing you wanted this meeting to be private, he offered to show my nephew around Headquarters."

So this woman was the victim's sister.... "What's his name?"

"Nicky."

The boy who haunted Vance's dreams now had a name. "How old is he?"

"He turned six three weeks ago. Were you the man in charge when my brother and sister-in-law were killed?"

"Yes. To tell you I'm sorry for what happened couldn't begin to convey my feelings."

The woman's gaze didn't flicker. "I won't even try to describe mine. Just tell me one thing. Was their accident preventable?"

"Yes," he answered without hesitation.

"In other words, the people working under you fell asleep on your watch and two lives were snuffed out as a result."

Hearing it put like that, he had to set the record straight. "My staff had nothing to do with it. I, myself, could have prevented the loss of life."

Ms. Darrow's expression hardened. "So you admit culpability."

"Yes. I take full blame."

A look of pain crossed over her features. "You can just stand there and admit it?" Her cry echoed that of his own tortured soul.

"Yes." He sucked in his breath.

"I work for a cruise line. Aboard ship, it's the captain's responsibility to maintain rigid safety regulations. If a disaster like that had happened while he was in charge he would have been relieved of his command and never given another ship again."

Rachel Darrow couldn't know she was preaching

to the converted. "If you've come to the park with the intention of bringing a lawsuit against me for negligence, maybe you should." It would only be what he deserved.

"Maybe I will."

In the next instant, she wheeled around and hurried out of his office. Vance could have gone after her, but it would cause a scene, something he was loath to do for a variety of reasons. In the first place, he needed to cool down before he approached her again.

The discovery of the Darrows' frozen bodies had affected every ranger in the park. A little boy had been orphaned—a boy whose aunt was all he had left.

* * * * *

Will Rachel allow Vance to explain—and will she let him into her heart?
Find out in
THE CHIEF RANGER
Available June 2009 from
Harlequin® American Romance®.

HARLEQUIN®
Romance®

COMING NEXT MONTH

Available June 9, 2009

#1566 A SMALL-TOWN HOMECOMING • Terry McLaughlin
Built to Last
The return of architect Tess Roussel to her hometown has put her on a collision course with John Jameson Quinn. The contractor has her reeling…his scandalous past overshadows everything. Tess wants to believe that the contractor is deserving of her professional admiration and her trust, but her love, too?

#1567 A HOLIDAY ROMANCE • Carrie Alexander
A summer holiday in the desert? What had Alice Potter been thinking? If it wasn't for resort manager Kyle Jarreau, her dream vacation would be a nightmare. But can they keep their fling a secret…? For Kyle's sake, they *have* to.

#1568 FROM FRIEND TO FATHER • Tracy Wolff
Reece Sandler never planned to raise his daughter with Sarah Martin. They were only friends when she agreed to be his surrogate. Now things have changed and they have to be parents—together. Fine. Easy. But only if Reece can control his attraction to Sarah.

#1569 BEST FOR THE BABY • Ann Evans
9 Months Later
Pregnant and alone, Alaina Tillman returns to Lake Harmony and Zack Davidson, her girlhood love. Yet as attracted as she is to him, life isn't just about the two of them anymore. She has to do what's best for her baby. Does that mean letting Zack in—or pushing him away?

#1570 NO ORDINARY COWBOY• Mary Sullivan
Home on the Ranch
A ranch is so not Amy Graves's scene. Still, she promised to help, so here she is. Funny thing is she starts to feel at home. And even funnier, she starts to fall for a cowboy—Hank Shelter. As she soon discovers, however, there's nothing ordinary about him.

#1571 ALL THAT LOVE IS • Ginger Chambers
Everlasting Love
Jillian Davis was prepared to walk away from her marriage. But when her husband, Brad, takes her on a shortcut, an accident nearly kills them. Now, with the SUV as their fragile shelter, Jillian's only hope lies with the man she was ready to leave behind forever.…

HSRCNMBPA0509